The Untold Story
of Princess Doe

Christie Leigh Napurano

To John & Lerma —

Best,

Christie

SDL Press
Hilton Head Island, S.C.

First Printing 2012

ISBN 978-0-9656589-6-6 (Hardcover)
ISBN 978-0-9656589-5-9 (Paperback)

Cover Photography:
Jaime Lyn Napurano

Cover Graphics:
SDL Press

Additional copies available for purchase.
Please send your inquiries to:

SDL Press
PO Box 198
Hawthorne, NJ 07507
(800) 468-2646
www.whoisprincessdoe.com

This book is dedicated to the memory of
Aunt Roz
1926-2011

Foreword

On July 15, 1982, the body of a young girl was found in the Cedar Ridge Cemetery in the small town of Blairstown, New Jersey. Her face had been mangled beyond recognition, her one-hundred-and-five-pound body discarded like trash. The grisly discovery was made by local workers at about eight o'clock in the morning, just on the southeast side of the cemetery, on a steep bank that overlooks the Paulinskill River.

Given the amount of time the body was exposed and the climate in the area at the time, the victim's age was approximated to be between fourteen and eighteen years old at the time of her death.

The citizens of Blairstown were horrified by the discovery in their safe, familiar town. They donated money for the unidentified girl to be buried in Cedar Ridge Cemetery, with a headstone marked "Princess Doe". Though the case garnered national media attention, the girl's identity was never determined, and her killer never found. The Princess Doe case was used as the impetus for recording unidentified murder victims into the National Crime Information Center (NCIC) database at the national level. It was the first such case entered by the FBI director, William H. Webster, in 1982.

There were numerous girls reported missing during that time period that were thought to be Princess Doe, but one by one they were ruled out due to dental records, DNA, and other forensic findings. The law enforcement officials working on the case came across several leads over the years, but eventually they all turned cold and the case remained unsolved.

In 1999, Princess Doe's body was exhumed in hopes of obtaining a better DNA sample. Unfortunately, no data exists to compare to the sample obtained from her remains.

Nearly thirty years after the body was found, Princess Doe's true identity remains a mystery and her killer has yet to be brought to justice. The narrative that follows is a fictional account that gives a name and a story to a girl who has been anonymous for far too long.

Meet The Martells

"**N**ow go in that room and don't come out until you think about what you've done!" her mother said, voice echoing down the hallway.

Julianne Martell stomped into her room and slammed her wooden door so she wouldn't have to hear her mother rant and rave and storm about the house. Julianne had long since concluded that her mother was insane, and she had just about had enough of her constant screaming and picking on her for every little thing she did. Julianne didn't think that coming home fifteen minutes past curfew was cause for the fireworks that were now going on, but with everything that had happened to their family in the past two years she knew her mother was losing it more and more with each passing day.

Julianne turned on her radio and tuned it to her favorite rock station. She didn't think it was fair of her mother to take everything out on her, especially when her older sister Amanda was hours late for her curfew even on school nights. At seventeen, Amanda was only two years older than Julianne, but she was out until the wee hours of the night, having sex with older boys and experimenting with drugs.

Julianne wished that her sister would have told her this information herself instead of her hearing it whispered as gossip amongst their high school peers, but Amanda only spoke to Julianne when she had to, and rarely about anything personal. Mostly she just pushed by her in the hallway at school and at home, and kicked her out of the bathroom whenever she needed to groom herself.

But Julianne still loved her sister and constantly prayed for her to change her wild ways. After all, Amanda was the only sister she had left.

Julianne could still hear Sandy Martell screaming and pacing around the kitchen, and then she heard what had become a very familiar sound – the sound of her mother slamming a cabinet door, loudly placing a glass on the counter, dropping ice cubes in it, and pouring a glass of vodka. Julianne shook her head and tears came to her eyes as she remembered what her family used to be like, in happier times, when they were normal and all together. Her mother knew she couldn't control Amanda; she was fearful that if she tried to exercise any kind of parental control, Amanda would be on the first train out of their small Long Island town. And after the double loss that had befallen them in recent years, Julianne knew that her mother would completely crumble if she lost anyone else whom she loved. Despite all their recent issues, she was sure that her mother still loved her and Amanda. She cranked her stereo louder and tried to drown out the sounds going on outside the safe haven of her bedroom.

Several minutes later there was a loud banging on the door. "It's God damn eleven at night, Julianne! Turn down that fucking radio before I come in there and throw it out the fucking window!" The doorknob jiggled clumsily and Julianne silently praised herself for remembering to lock the door. "Do you hear me in there? I'm sick and tired of your bullshit! I'm your mother and you'd better listen to me, God damn it!"

Julianne reached over without moving from her spot on the bed and clicked the radio off completely. She had had enough of this day. And of most of the days that had preceded it, for that matter. She carefully got under the covers and closed her eyes but was mindful not to fall asleep just yet. She never fell asleep before she made sure that she heard Amanda stumble into the house and go in her room.

Unfortunately Amanda hadn't made an appearance until almost five in the morning over the course of the past few nights, so Julianne was exhausted from waiting up for her. Sandy didn't know that Amanda was keeping these late hours, because she usually passed out long before her daughter got home. When Amanda first started ignoring her mother's wishes and staying out much later than she should have, her mother would get in the car in the early morning hours and drive from house to house and parking lot to parking lot searching for her. She found her a couple of times, and the fight between Amanda and her mother that would follow these discoveries was usually ugly and often involved Julianne breaking up a fist fight between the remaining two members of her family. Then one night about six months ago, her mother had gotten in the car after several glasses of vodka and was pulled over. The policeman that pulled her over had been a friend of Julianne's father and took pity on his old friend's wife and let her go with a warning – but told her that she was no longer allowed to drive after nine in the evening. After that incident, her mother started to drink even more and rarely got in the car at all since she had quit her job months ago and really had nowhere else to go.

Julianne drifted off into a fitful sleep, dreaming the same dream that she had been having for months. She dreamt of a time not that long ago, when her family was intact and happy. These were the only memories that Julianne had, and as much as they upset her they were also all she had to hold onto of the normal life she once led.

* * *

The Martells had, at one time, been the typical all-American nuclear family. Alan Martell had married his high school sweetheart Sandra in an elaborate ceremony in the Hamptons. Both Alan and Sandy came from old money, and Sandy's family had spared no expense for their only daughter's wedding. Their union made headlines in the local paper because of the high-society guest list, and it was one of the most lavish and expensive weddings to happen on Long Island in years. After the wedding, the Martells settled in a small town on Long Island about thirty minutes outside of Manhattan, because Alan worked in the city as one of the top traders on Wall Street. Even though they didn't need the money, Sandy got a part-time job as a receptionist at the dentist's office in their town, just to keep busy. On her days off she volunteered at various battered women's shelters in the area, but made sure she was home in time every night to cook dinner for her husband.

The Martells were incredibly well liked and respected in their small town of Haverford, Long Island. Since both Alan and Sandy had no siblings, they relied on the company of their neighbors and colleagues, and had many close family friends as a result of their parents' social status.

Sadly, about a year and a half after Alan and Sandy's marriage, Alan's parents were killed while boating off of the Long Island Sound. It was the day after a hurricane had passed along the East Coast, and there were warnings not to take watercraft out, but Alan's father was an experienced boater and was confident he could handle their cruiser. He had been planning this boat trip with two other couples for months, and didn't want to miss his chance to show off his new boat, so he insisted that the excursion not be cancelled. Unfortunately Mr. Martell was unaware of a major undercurrent that swept them far out to sea where they eventually ran out of gas. They were missing for twelve days before the Coast Guard finally found the boat hundreds of miles off shore in the Atlantic. Onboard they found the bodies of three women – Alan's mother, and the two other wives who had gone on the trip. They had died from exposure to the elements and starvation. The surrounding area was searched for weeks after but there was never a trace of Alan's father or the other two men. It was speculated that the men had probably taken the blow-up emergency raft and tried to row back to safety…but simply got lost at sea.

The loss of Alan's parents completely devastated him, and he had taken a year off from work to deal with it. His parents were the only family he had, aside from a few random cousins and aunts and uncles who he wasn't close with at all. After his parents passed on, he barely kept in touch with any other family members, aside from Christmas cards. Sandy didn't know what to do for her husband other than be with him at all times. She, too, quit her job and devoted herself to waiting on Alan hand and foot. As if they weren't close enough already, Alan and Sandy became almost like one person. They never appeared in public without each other, and even their daily activities were done together – from cooking breakfast to doing laundry to showering together. Sandy's parents did not approve of this reclusiveness, and in turn Sandy became more and more distant from them. Since she had no brothers or sisters either, it was easy for her to become more and more dependent on Alan for everything.

Sandy eventually convinced Alan that the only way they would ever feel whole again was to start a family of their own. They had always wanted to have children and were just about ready before the incident with Alan's parents happened. So, once Alan was feeling somewhat alright again, they began to plan the newest addition to the Martell clan.

Sarah Jean Martell was born on March 13, 1960. She was an angelic looking baby, with beautiful blue eyes and golden curls that would have made Cupid jealous. Everyone said she was the spitting image of her father, and she truly was Daddy's little girl. Alan and Sandy doted on Sarah Jean, giving her everything that she could have possibly wanted – and even everything that she didn't want. Since Alan inherited all of his parents' fortune when they died, there was nothing that any of the Martells would ever want again, that was for certain. Sarah Jean was so beautiful that one of Sandy's friends convinced her to take the little girl into the city for baby modeling. Sarah Jean became an instant miniature celebrity, appearing in nationwide commercials and magazine ads in *Vogue* and *McCall's*.

Alan and Sandy were so overjoyed with their daughter and her success that they wanted to expand their happy little brood and give Sarah Jean a sibling. Three years later, Sandy gave birth to another little girl – Amanda Sue. But as lovely and docile as Sarah Jean was, Amanda was the complete opposite. She was up, crying all night, and Alan and Sandy were beside themselves trying to get her to stop. She had a horrible case of colic and rarely ate or slept. Alan and Sandy took her to doctor after doctor to try to find a cure for her misery, but to no avail. Sandy tried to get Amanda into commercials and print ads like Sarah Jean, but Amanda rarely smiled and wouldn't sit still long enough to get her photo taken. Sandy contemplated pulling Sarah Jean out of the business because bringing Amanda into the city several times a week was a nightmare. She knew that Sarah Jean enjoyed modeling so much she couldn't bear to have two unhappy children. So she hired a nanny who stayed home and watched Amanda while Sandy took Sarah Jean into the city day after day.

By the time Sarah Jean was five and Amanda was two, Sandy was pregnant again. Julianne May Martell came into the world on a crisp October afternoon, and upon her birth, Alan commented, "My life is finally complete. I have three wonderful daughters and the most perfect wife in the entire world." Sandy smiled and kissed the forehead of her sleeping two-hour-old daughter and thought how lucky she was to have Alan and her girls.

Life passed rather uneventfully for the Martells for the next decade. Sarah Jean started school, Amanda grew up and stopped being difficult, and Julianne was the sweet baby of the family. In 1975, Sandy's mother passed away. Just eight months later, her father died of a broken heart. Although Sandy had been estranged from her parents for some time, she was still devastated over losing them. Sarah Jean, Amanda, and Julianne attended both services and put on somber little faces but weren't really in mourning because they didn't know their grandparents well at all. Sandy was shocked when she found out that her parents left everything to her; she thought for sure they would have left it to other extended family or even the hired help before they would have left it to her. It drove her mad with guilt to know that even though she and her parents had grown apart, they still loved her enough to leave her a small fortune, and she cursed herself for being so stubborn for so many years. After the loss of Sandy's parents and her subsequent inheritance, the Martells moved to the nicer town of Carrollton, south of where they were currently living.

The Martells had grown up to be three lovely teenage girls. Sarah Jean, at eighteen, still had the model looks that had earned her so much reverence when she was a baby. Her soft blonde hair fell just below her shoulders, and her sparkling blue eyes constantly danced with excitement. Her figure was perfect, and she was the envy of most girls at her high school, especially when she was voted Homecoming Queen. Boys were constantly calling the house wanting to take her out on dates, but Alan Martell would have none of that. "We're a respectable family," he would say, "nobody dates until I think they are ready." Sarah Jean had been accepted to college in Vermont, and Julianne had not only grown into the spitting image of her eldest sister, but revered her and mimicked her every move. Alan and Sandy called her "Mini Sarah", and she loved it. She wanted nothing more than to do everything just like her sister. Despite their age gap, Sarah Jean and Julianne were very close. They were always playing card games and jumping rope together, and Sarah Jean would always help Julianne with her homework when she was stuck. Although she was only thirteen, it was clear that Julianne was destined to be a definite beauty just like her older sister.

Fifteen-year-old Amanda had a darker shade of blonde hair than Sarah Jean, and her eyes were a pretty grey. Amanda ruined her looks though, by dressing in unflattering colors and clothes, and wearing way too much makeup. Her sisters and mother tried to tell her this, but when they realized it only made her efforts to look bad increase, they left it alone. Amanda was more withdrawn than her sisters, often acting out in school by getting bad grades and getting into fights with other students. Alan and Sandy were concerned about her, but chalked it up to harmless teenage behavior.

The day that Sarah Jean left for college was what Julianne thought to be the saddest day of her life. It was as if her best friend had left. For weeks, she moped around the house, only perking up when she received letters from Sarah Jean in the mail. Sandy felt for her daughter, and dared to hope that Julianne and Amanda might some day have the same close-knit relationship, but that would have to wait until Amanda was done going through her tumultuous phase. She often tried to orchestrate outings for Amanda and Julianne, but to no avail. Amanda would either not show up, or throw such a fit about going somewhere with the family, that Sandy had no choice but to leave her at home.

With Sarah Jean gone, Sandy and Alan took more notice of Amanda's actions and realized that there might be a bigger problem than they had originally thought. Amanda would come home glassy eyed and completely out of it, and one night when Alan questioned her she locked herself in the bathroom and threatened to slit her wrists if he didn't leave her alone. Several days later, Amanda was hauled off to a therapist (under the premise that Sandy was taking her to the mall) and began intense therapy. The therapist concluded that Amanda was depressed, and put her on medication to ease her pain.

Alan and Sandy were beside themselves. What could they have possibly done wrong to make their daughter so angry and self-destructive? They tried to think of what could have gone wrong but came up with nothing, until the day that Amanda's therapist told them that Amanda felt that they loved Sarah Jean more than her.

Sandy was so consumed with guilt that she herself became depressed. She was devastated at the thought that she had played favorites with one of her daughters, and vowed to somehow make it up to Amanda. One day she went out and shopped for Amanda all day, and came home with thousands of dollars worth of clothes and makeup for her. Amanda was actually gracious when she accepted Sandy's gifts, and Sandy was ecstatic when she saw Amanda wearing the tasteful clothes and makeup she had picked out, instead of her normal unflattering attire.

After several months of medication, therapy, and non-stop attention from her parents, Amanda seemed to have turned her life around. She stopped hanging out with her destructive friends, and started treating Julianne with more respect. Julianne was shocked but pleased on the day that Amanda came into her room and asked her to play cards.

By the time Sarah Jean came home from college for the summer, Amanda was a completely different person. She was more the type of daughter that the Martells wanted to have; more like Sarah Jean and Julianne. She was respectful, well-groomed, and engaging. The sisters now all played games and spent their time together. Alan and Sandy were so pleased that they took a month long vacation to Europe with the girls that summer, to celebrate the change in their family dynamic.

When they returned, Sarah Jean skipped off to college to begin her second year, and Amanda began looking into which college she wanted to attend. Julianne was now Amanda's shadow, helping her write letters to schools requesting information and applications. Alan and Sandy were happier than ever, both with their relationship and with the way they had raised their three model children.

And then one day, all five of their lives changed forever.

* * *

Julianne would never forget that day. It was an unusually cold Tuesday in late March, and the telephone rang rather early in the morning. Alan had already left for work, and Amanda and Julianne were sitting at the breakfast table enjoying scrambled eggs and toast. Sandy, clad in a silk robe and curlers, innocently picked up the phone and said, "Hello, Martell residence."

Before Julianne knew what was happening, she heard a scream and a crash and turned around to see her mother drop the phone and fall to the floor in a dead faint. Amanda sprang into action, jumping up and grabbing the phone from her mother's hand, saying, "Hello? Hello?"

Julianne tended to her mother, bringing her a cold washcloth to put on her face and a larger towel to put between her head and the tile floor. As Julianne caressed her mother's face with the wet washcloth, she looked up to see if Amanda was getting any information from whoever was on the other end of that phone call. What she saw worried her.

Amanda's face had completely drained of all color, and she was breathing heavily while trying to keep it together pretending to be Sandy. She kept saying things like, "What? How could this...? What can we...? What have you...?" Finally she took a deep breath and said, "I'll have my husband call you," and hung up without saying goodbye.

She looked down at Julianne on the floor, staring up at her with her curious blue eyes that so resembled Sarah Jean's. "Sarah Jean is missing," Amanda blurted out, and then began bawling.

*Missing....Missing...Sarah Jean is missing...*Julianne heard the haunting words echo hollowly in her mind as she came out of her dream to the sound of the table in their foyer crashing to the ground and a voice croaking, "Shit."

Sisterly Love

J ulianne sighed and got out of bed to help Amanda. She glanced at her clock as she trudged out of her bedroom. A quarter past five in the morning. What could Amanda possibly have been doing until this ungodly hour? She prayed that her sister was unharmed, and also that she hadn't woken Sandy, who was passed out on the couch. Otherwise, it would undoubtedly send her mother into another drunken tirade.

Coming down the stairs into the foyer, Julianne saw Amanda bending over trying to right the table, not realizing that she had completely snapped one of its legs right in half. Amanda's pale white bottom was hanging out of the back of her short pleated skirt. Her legs looked like two toothpicks that seemed to go on for days. The dark blue shirt showed off her flat stomach, as well as the better half of her breasts. Julianne thought she looked much skinnier than she had in recent months, but decided not to mention it.

"Mandy," Julianne said gently. "It broke. See? Don't worry about it, I'll fix it tomorrow. Let's go upstairs."

Amanda looked up at her younger sister's calm face with a scowl. "Fuck you, Sarah Jean," she spat in Julianne's face. "Leave me the fuck alone. I fucking hate you. We all fucking hate you."

Julianne could smell the alcohol and pot as well as another unfamiliar substance strongly emanating from her sister. She pursed her lips and fought back the tears that stung her eyes and tried again. "Amanda, it's me, Julianne. Let me take you upstairs, please?"

Amanda licked her lips and said, "I need a glass of water."

Julianne left her sister in the foyer and retreated to the kitchen to get Amanda a glass of water. As she handed it to Amanda, she saw tears streaking down her sister's face.

"What's the matter, Mandy?" Julianne asked softly.

Amanda gulped down the glass of water loudly and with a sniffle looked up at Julianne. Amanda swatted aimlessly at her sister, which caused one of her breasts to fall out of her top entirely. Julianne could only imagine the scene her sister had made at whatever party she had been at earlier in the evening.

"I'm fucked up," she said, her voice threatening to break at any moment. "And you, Sarah Jean, messed it all up."

To anyone else, Amanda wouldn't have been making a bit of sense. But Julianne knew exactly what she was talking about. In Amanda's drunken stupors, she often mistook Julianne for Sarah Jean, and would carry on about how much she hated her, how happy they all were before she went missing, and how Sarah Jean's disappearance caused her to go back to her old wild ways. Her confusion greatly upset Julianne, who was torn between hate for the sister she would never see again because of her stupidity and bad choices; but also loyalty to Sarah Jean, who she still resembled in every way, shape, and form. Julianne still tried to emulate everything Sarah Jean had been before she disappeared. She wanted to hate Sarah Jean, because it would make so many things much easier – but on the other hand, she just couldn't.

Julianne kneeled down next to her quietly weeping sister and stroked her face. "Amanda, it's Julianne. Come on upstairs; let me put you to sleep. It's very late."

Julianne wasn't sure if Amanda was too drunk to argue or if she actually understood what was being said, but after another drunken scowl in Julianne's direction, she picked herself up off the floor and allowed herself to be led upstairs. As they passed by Sandy, who was passed out and snoring loudly on the couch, Amanda pointed to her and said, "Bitch." Julianne chose to ignore this rather common outburst and said yet another silent prayer that Sandy had drunk just enough vodka to keep her sleeping for another few hours.

Julianne picked up the pajamas she had laid out for Amanda and helped her dress and get into bed. "J'lanne?" Amanda slurred as her sister started creeping out the door. Julianne turned around.

"Yes, Mandy?"

"C'you gemme another glassa water? Plitty please? Love you."

After Julianne had gotten her sister another glass of water, she returned to her bed, which had seemed so much more comfortable when she had gotten into it before. She tossed and turned and cried softly for the family she had once known, and for what they had become.

In the morning, Julianne was the first one to wake up. This was not unusual. Both her mother and sister were usually too busy nursing hangovers to get out of bed right away, so she made a pot of coffee for them and set out some bread next to the toaster for when they woke up. She then decided to go for a run.

Running was Julianne's favorite part of the day. It gave her a chance to breathe, and to be out of the toxic atmosphere of her own home. It gave her a chance to see birds, and trees, and neighbors who had long since stopped calling on her family. She kind of hoped that her daily run through the neighborhood would let their community know that they hadn't all gone completely off the deep end. Julianne ran over a wooden bridge and stopped to look over into the babbling river below. She was momentarily shocked when she thought she saw Sarah Jean's face smiling back at her. She shook her head, closed her eyes and looked again, realizing that it was only her own face that she was seeing. Several tears trickled down her cheek and into the water, and then Julianne was off and running again.

She longed for a different life, one far away from the hell that she had come to know in the past few years. She knew that she would have to leave eventually, that her sanity depended upon it. But being only fifteen years old, she had limited resources and experience to plan her escape. Julianne knew that there was still a lot of money in her mother's account; she was the one to open the bank statements when they came every month. What she didn't know was how to get the money out without actually having her mother go to the bank to withdraw it for her. She knew that the only time Sandy went to the bank to take out cash was when she needed money for more alcohol, and she usually took out way more than she needed. Julianne wondered in her daydreams what would happen if she could get her hands on enough of the cash in the account to skip town and set up a nice life for herself, and maybe Amanda too.

Julianne also didn't know how much it would actually cost her to get out of town, much less the mode of transportation in which she would do so. She knew there was a train somewhere nearby, but she also knew that it only went into New York City. Did she want to go to New York City? She wasn't really sure. Julianne had heard lots of unpleasant things about young girls who went to New York City by themselves, and she didn't want to end up a statistic. She just wanted another life, far away from Long Island, and far away from anyone who had ever known her family.

Julianne was so lost in thought that she didn't even see the man before she ran right into him.

"I'm so sorry!" she breathed in horror, looking at the young man in front of her picking himself up off the pavement. Her initial reaction when he looked into her eyes was that of attraction; he was tall and good looking, with light brown hair and the same piercing blue eyes as her.

"That's OK," he said good-naturedly, brushing himself off. "I wish cute girls would run into me all the time."

Julianne blushed a scarlet red and looked down at her feet. He was definitely older than she, though probably not by much, but definitely older (and not to mention more experienced) if he was blatantly hitting on her after meeting her less than a minute ago.

"Shy, are we?" he asked. "What's your name?"

Julianne looked back up into his welcoming face and replied hesitantly, "Um, Julie...uh, Mar...um, Martin. Julie Martin."

She wasn't exactly sure why she had lied about her last name. She had no idea who this stranger was, but she did know that she didn't want him putting two and two together and realizing that she was a member of the tainted Martell family of Carrollton lore.

"Well hello, Julie Martin. I'm Stan Douglas," he said, extending his hand to shake hers.

Julianne smiled and shook his hand. He was even cuter when he smiled.

"Are you from around here?"

"No," Stan admitted. "I'm from New Jersey, actually."

Julianne was immediately interested. She had never been to New Jersey, but had heard nice things about the state that was just beyond New York City. She put it at the top of her list of places to run away to.

"So....what are you doing here?" Julianne asked boldly.

"Aren't we full of questions, Miss Martin," Stan said with a grin. "I'm visiting my aunt and uncle, they live just down the street."

Julianne was instantly glad she had lied about her name. Even though Julianne Martell and Julie Martin sounded similar, she was sure it would take at least a little while for Stan's aunt and uncle to figure out who she was.

"Got a few minutes to sit down and talk?" Stan gestured to a bench several yards away. "I'm giving myself a tour of my aunt and uncle's town and the surrounding area because they're busy all day, so I'm all alone and don't know where the hot spots in town are..."

His tone was suggestive; a little too suggestive for Julianne's liking. She glanced around, saw no other signs of life, and suddenly remembered that she was a fifteen-year-old girl talking to a strange boy who she had just met that was coming on to her. Her boldness suddenly disappeared and she took a step backward.

"I...I have to get home, actually," Julianne stammered. "My father doesn't really like me to talk to boys that I don't really know." It wasn't exactly a lie – Julianne was sure that that was something her father would have said, if he were still around. She thought Stan would be offended, but he just gave her a toothy grin and said, "Alright. Hope I don't get lost out here all by myself. Maybe I'll run into you again, Julie Martin."

Julianne gave him a quick wave and a half smile and turning around, began running in the direction of her home. She turned around briefly to see if he was following her, or at least still looking at her, but he had walked off in the other direction.

A feeling of dread had settled in Julianne's stomach, but it had nothing to do with Stan Douglas. She always got that feeling when she was headed back in the direction of her house...basically because she never knew what she was walking back into. She tried to slow her pace down so as to prolong her time out of the house as she got closer to 21 Senderfill Road, but she inevitably found herself opening the front door to the unknown.

Surprisingly, the house was rather quiet. "Mom?" she called out into the stale air. "Amanda?" But there was no answer. Julianne walked up the stairs, continuing to call out for her mother and sister, praying that nothing bad had happened to them.

She briefly paused at the first door at the top of the stairs, which was not only closed but had not been opened in so long that the doorknob had a thin layer of dust on it. Julianne wondered when the last time anyone had even been inside Sarah Jean's room. She knew that she hadn't gone in there in almost six months, and she could guarantee that it had been even longer for her mother and Amanda.

Julianne gently turned the silver doorknob and the door creaked open. Sarah Jean's bedroom was like a museum – a very dusty, cobweb-filled museum – but everything was just exactly as she had left it. From her diary on her desk with a pen on top of it, to a few pairs of slacks draped over the edge of her bed, it almost felt that Sarah Jean was going to walk back in the door any minute, like the past year had just been a big joke or a dream. Julianne sat down at her sister's desk and looked at a picture in a frame that brought fresh tears to her eyes. It was a picture of the two of them, looking practically identical, the day that Sarah Jean left for college. Stuck in the corner of the frame was a school photo of Amanda, with her snarky smile and crazy makeup. Julianne marveled at her sister's ability to include Amanda in everything even when she was most awful to Sarah Jean. The day that they got the news began to replay itself again, as it so often did, in Julianne's mind....

* * *

Her mother had hit the floor and gone unconscious after talking to the college representative on the phone. Julianne's mind began racing. Missing? What did that mean? Where had she gone? How long had she been gone? This had to be some kind of joke. Sarah Jean wouldn't have run away. Julianne knew above all that her sister was very happy and content with her very charmed life and would have no want or reason to be elsewhere. And who could have possibly taken her? She was a good student, a smart girl. She wouldn't have done anything that would have gotten her into any trouble. No, the college must have made a mistake. Her sister could not be missing, it was just impossible. She was due to come home for the summer in just another month and a half, and she and Julianne had planned a day trip to the beach for the first hot day of the season.

"Amanda," Julianne said, standing up to grab her sister, who had started shaking violently while sobbing. "Amanda, what's going on? What do you mean, missing?"

Amanda gulped and tried to speak between sobs. "College...they said her room...roommate was out at her boyfriend's...no one has seen her...don't know how it happened....not showing up to clas-ses....Daddy. Call Daddy."

Julianne looked at her mother still passed out on the floor. Her breathing was becoming shallow, and her face was getting pale. Amanda knelt down next to her and sobbed in her face. "Mommy, Mommy," she cried, but Sandy didn't stir. Julianne somehow main-tained her calm and picked up the phone and called her father's office.

"May I speak to Alan Martell please?" she asked the secretary when she picked up, her voice sounding very small. The minute she heard her father's baritone, however, she completely lost it. "Daddy!" she shrieked. "Sarah Jean is missing! The college called and Mommy fainted and Amanda won't stop crying. Should I call 911? Daddy, please help us, what should I do?"

Julianne didn't hear anything her father said. Before she knew it she was wailing to a dial tone, and she didn't even have the strength to hang up the phone. She fell to the floor, still clutching the phone, and watched through bleary, tear-filled eyes, as Amanda clung to their mother. She hoped her father was on his way home because she didn't know how to deal with anything that was going on at the moment.

Julianne was never exactly sure how much time had passed before what happened next. She remembered kneeling down on the floor to try and comfort her sister and revive her mother, and the next thing she remembered was her father busting in the front door of the house screaming, "Sandra? Girls? Where are you? What's going on?"

The minute they saw their father's frame appear in the kitchen doorway, Amanda and Julianne ran to him and clung to his legs, sobbing. Sandy had come to, but was sitting on the kitchen floor in a fetal position, her back against the wall, clinging to her bent knees. Alan immediately ran to his wife and picked her up in his arms, caressing her face and repeating, "Sandy, Sandy, honey," while struggling to fight back tears of his own.

Julianne didn't know how long that was happening for, but eventually she saw her mother's eyes flutter and focus on Alan's face and she breathed a small sigh of relief. "Where is my Sarah Jean?" Sandy asked immediately.

Alan Martell cleared his throat and said, "Honey, you fainted and the girls called me at work. I just got here. I'm going to call the college back and find out exactly what is going on. In the meantime, I need you to go in the other room and book us four plane tickets to Vermont immediately."

"But where...?" Sandy said, dazed. "Alan...my baby...why..."

While all this was going on, Amanda started sobbing again, loudly, which caused Sandy to break down in great heaving sobs. Julianne knew what she had to do. She quietly slipped out of the kitchen, grabbing her father's wallet off the counter as she exited. She went into Alan's office and picked up the phone, waiting for a dial tone. Julianne called information and got herself connected to American Airlines, then in her best grown up voice told the woman on the other line that she was Sandy Martell and she needed to book four tickets to Burlington, Vermont as soon as possible. The woman on the phone was more than pleasant as Julianne carefully repeated the numbers off her father's credit card and spelled out the names of all her family members. The woman said that there were four tickets waiting for them at the American Airlines counter in the airport and their flight was leaving at seven that evening. Julianne quietly thanked the woman and hung up the phone. She returned to the kitchen to report that she had completed the task of getting flights for the family.

When she walked into the kitchen, her father was on the phone, and her mother was sitting in a chair listening intently to her husband's conversation while Amanda patted her head with a damp towel and wiped away her own silent tears.

"I'm not sure I understand," Alan was saying calmly, but Julianne could tell he was close to breaking down. "So you're telling me that my daughter, a straight A student with dozens of friends just disappeared and you waited *two days* to call her family? What kind of people do you have working for you up there? Don't you think we should have been contacted when she didn't show up for the first class?" Alan Martell knew how unreasonable this sounded. Kids with colds might not show up for class. But Julianne could tell he didn't care.

He paused, frowning, then shook his head. "Do you know who you're talking about? This is Sarah Jean Martell for Christ's sake. She's never done anything bad in her life, she would never run away. Don't

even tell me that you think you know my daughter better than I do..."
Another pause, and Julianne saw her father's face getting red and
twisted with rage.

"What kind of a place are you running up there? I expect better
treatment and better care for my daughter than this! I don't give a
flying shit how many students you have to keep an eye on, I sent my
daughter to your establishment because you told me you prided
yourself on individualized treatment of students. Is this what you call
preferential treatment? My family and I are on the next flight up
there, as soon as I make flight plans –"

"I did it, Daddy. We leave at seven tonight," Julianne piped up.
Alan glanced at his daughter with a slightly shocked look, but was
too enraged to say anything to her, so he continued, " —which have
already been made. We will see you tonight. And I don't care what
time we get there, you better be sitting in your office waiting for me
because I'm coming to *you* first." And with that he slammed the
phone down with an angry click.

He turned to Julianne and his expression softened. "Thank you,
baby," he said, and without any words other than that he muttered,
"Let's pack."

Julianne looked at her mother who was still staring off into noth-
ingness, her face streaked with mascara and tears, and Amanda, who
looked like a frightened little animal. Alan paced once around the
kitchen and then stormed out, presumably to pack.

Julianne looked at Amanda and said, "Mandy, you stay with
Mommy. I'll put some stuff in a bag for you and her."

"We should change her clothes," Amanda sniffled. Julianne nodded, walked out, and returned several minutes later with a pair of

pants and a sweatshirt of her mother's. Amanda began to help her mother undress, and as Julianne took the curlers out of her mother's hair she stared at the faraway look in Sandy's eyes. She wondered where Sarah Jean was and if anyone in their family would ever be right again. She wanted so badly to stay there with her mother, but she knew what she had to do. Once again Julianne left the kitchen and went into her room to pack a bag for her and Amanda.

* * *

As the daymare faded away, Julianne shook her head and realized that she had tiny tears dribbling down her cheeks. She looked again at the picture of Sarah Jean on her desk, and touched it with her index finger and said, "I miss you, my favorite sister." Then she got up silently and exited her sister's room, carefully closing the door behind her. As she turned around to walk down the hallway, she saw Amanda at the other end of the hall, with a plastic bag in her hand and a scowl on her face.

"What are you doing in there?" Amanda snapped.

"I...I just...I don't know," Julianne admitted. As she looked into Amanda's seemingly soulless eyes, she felt a wave of emotion come over her, and wished to God that Amanda would just feel a bit of remorse and loss for Sarah Jean with her right then. "I miss her, Mandy. Don't you?"

Amanda didn't skip a beat. "No fucking way," she spat. "She didn't give a shit about us, and I don't give a shit about her. If she did, she never would have made the stupid decision to fucking walk around alone in the middle of the night and get herself snatched."

And with that she pushed past Julianne and slammed the bathroom door.

Julianne got a quick glimpse of what Amanda had in the plastic bag, and if she was close to breaking down before, one look at that and she completely lost it. A pregnancy test. Amanda was taking a pregnancy test. Julianne ran to her room and buried her face in her pillow and howled long guttural screams that echoed down the hallway, down the stairs, and throughout the house.

Eventually Julianne's screams woke Sandy Martell up, who stood up from the couch and immediately grabbed her face due to a screaming headache. She stumbled to the kitchen and gulped down a glass of water and shot down five aspirin. Hearing Julianne's screams from upstairs caused her head to pound harder, and she screamed as loud as she could muster, "Shut *up*, Julianne! Holy shit, why are you so loud?"

Julianne didn't even hear her mother. She continued to sob as if it were just yesterday that they had found out the news about Sarah Jean. She couldn't believe that Amanda would say such a thing about Sarah Jean, and she knew that she didn't mean it. She knew that Amanda was just as hurt as she was about everything that had happened; and she refused to believe that what Amanda had said was even true. Sarah Jean's friends had said that they had all been out at a party and Sarah Jean suddenly wasn't there, they didn't know where she had gone, she just left by herself, or with a guy, they weren't really sure.

And what the hell was Amanda doing with a pregnancy test? Julianne's mind swirled with dread and fear. Amanda couldn't be pregnant. Julianne knew she was somewhat promiscuous, but she always hoped that Amanda was smart enough to be careful…she didn't even think Amanda had a boyfriend.

But before Julianne could speculate any further about Amanda, her bedroom door flung open and Sandy stood there in a hung-over rage. Her eyes were bloodshot and her sallow skin seemed to hang off of her sad, aging face. She wheezed a few times before finally opening her mouth to scold her daughter.

"What is wrong with you?" she shouted at Julianne. "It's so God damn early in the morning and you're waking everyone up!"

"It's almost eleven!" Julianne wailed, not even caring what the consequences could be for talking back to her mother. "Why don't you try waking up at a normal hour like a normal mother?"

Before she knew what was happening, Julianne was shielding herself against sporadic blows from her mother. "I'll *kill you* if you talk back to me!" Sandy shrieked, hitting Julianne with angry fists. "Don't you ever tell me what to do! I'm your fucking mother!"

As the beating session was going on, Amanda walked by Julianne's room and glanced inside. Julianne saw a flash of pity in her sister's eyes, and doing probably the most decent thing she had done in months, she interfered, pulling Sandy off Julianne as the three of them screamed.

"Mother!" Amanda said. "Stop it!"

"She's disrespectful and she deserves everything she gets!" Sandy croaked, her voice destroyed from months of drinking and chain smoking.

"Ma, you're really going to hurt her! Stop it! Mother!" Amanda said again, grabbing at her mother's arms and yanking her to the floor. Julianne continued to bury her face in her pillow and wail, wishing that she was anywhere but there at that moment. Sandy, defeated, sat on the floor and put her hands up to her ears trying to drown out Julianne's cries. Amanda stood there, mediating, making sure Sandy didn't go back at Julianne. Eventually Sandy stood up and made her way out of Julianne's bedroom. The two sisters heard the door to the master bedroom slam shut and Julianne stopped crying for a minute and picked up her head, looking at Amanda with puffy eyes.

"Thank you," she mumbled, while Amanda stood there and looked at her, expressionless.

"You should know better," Amanda scolded quietly. "You know she doesn't feel well."

Julianne felt a surge of anger, and shot back, "She never feels well. Maybe she should stop drinking for a day or two."

Amanda stared at Julianne, twisting her mouth into a disappointing frown. "We all have our own way of dealing with shit," she said, and turned to walk away. Julianne stopped her.

"Are you?" she whispered quietly.

"What?" Amanda asked, spinning around.

"I saw what you had in that bag," Julianne said, lowering her eyes. "Are you?"

Amanda paused for a long moment. "Not this time," she said. "Thankfully." And with that she was gone.

Julianne and Stan

J ulianne breathed a long sigh of relief and lay back down in her
bed. At least that was one less thing she had to worry about for
the time being. Several minutes later she picked up her head and
looked at the clock. She groaned softly when she realized she had to
be at work in less than an hour. Julianne had a part time job at the
local ice cream parlor, scooping cups and cones for a measly three
dollars and ten cents an hour. She despised the job, but was somewhat proud because she had gotten it entirely on her own. Even
though she and Amanda had tried to access their parents' account
months ago (especially because their father had made it clear that he
took not a cent when he left) and knew if they did they would have as
much money as they wanted, Julianne felt that it was a good move to
have a job of her own. She sometimes cringed when she got her
paycheck, thinking of all the hours she had put in that week compared to the scant figure she looked at on the check, but a part of her
felt proud and independent. Julianne cashed every check and put all
the money in a jar under her bed.

Begrudgingly, she tore herself out of bed and began to get ready
for work. It was a good thirty minute walk away, but Julianne didn't

mind. As usual, as long as she was out of her house, she didn't care where she was going.

Upon arriving at work, her boss was in a bit of a mood. He looked at Julianne with beady eyes as she took her place behind the counter, and said, "Julianne, the soft ice cream maker isn't working. We're trying to fix it, but in the meantime just tell customers that we're temporarily out of soft ice cream."

Julianne nodded in consent and put on her dingy red apron that read "Seth's Ice Cream" and began helping the customers that were in line. The next two hours passed rather uneventfully until the door chimes sounded and none other than Stan Douglas walked through the front door. Julianne stared at him with excitement, realizing that he was not as old as she had originally thought.

Catching herself staring, Julianne immediately looked down, avoiding eye contact. She was embarrassed to have a job; most of the teenagers in her town were wealthy enough that they could do without. But Stan didn't know her situation and why she desperately longed to be anywhere but the place she had to call her home.

Eventually he noticed her while glancing at the ice cream flavors, and said, "Hey, Julie, is that you?"

Julianne started to blush and stared at her feet. Her co-worker Katherine nudged her and said, "Jule, he's talking to you."

Julianne obliged and walked over to the section of the counter where Stan was standing, giving her that huge grin that he had worn earlier that morning. "Well, well," he said, "Look who it is. I didn't know you had a job here."

With a sudden burst of courage, Julianne said, "I didn't know you were so intent on finding me."

Stan threw his head back and laughed. He had nice teeth, Julianne thought. She was completely drawn to his blue eyes and infectious laughter, and found herself laughing along with him. Stan made Julianne's body tingle in places it had never tingled before.

"So what's good here?" he asked her.

"Well," she said wryly, "Our soft ice cream is usually the best, but the machine is broken."

"I knew I should have gone to the ice cream place down the road," Stan joked.

"But then you wouldn't have found me," Julianne said boldly. She couldn't believe she was carrying on with this flirtatious banter, but somehow she found herself intrigued by Stan and the way she felt when he was around her.

"This is true," Stan said seriously. "Well, then I guess I'll just have a small chocolate cone. Think you could throw some sprinkles on there for me, or would that be too much trouble?"

"Rainbow or chocolate?" Julianne asked with mock professionalism.

"Why, rainbow, of course," Stan answered.

Julianne made Stan's order with an air of excitement, and even gave him extra sprinkles. She had never experimented with boys before, and she didn't understand the rush of emotions she was feeling having him there, but she liked it.

As she handed him his chocolate ice cream, he asked, "What time are you done?" Julianne looked at the clock, and then hesitated. She didn't want to end up like Amanda, or worse, Sarah Jean. But her emotions got the best of her and she answered confidently, "Two hours. Eight o'clock."

"Want to hang out after?" Stan asked.

"I should really go home, my mother will wonder where I am," Julianne lied, knowing that there was really only a fifty-fifty chance that Sandy would be coherent enough to realize that she wasn't home before her curfew.

"Well then how about I meet you back here and walk you home?" Stan suggested. Before she could stop herself, Julianne felt herself nodding in agreement. "OK," she said. "I'll see you in two hours." How much trouble could she get into walking home with Stan? If he tried to pull anything, she figured she could just run away.

Stan smiled, waved goodbye, and walked out the chiming doors. The next two hours seemed to be the longest hours in Julianne's life, but before she knew it she was cleaning off the counters and walking out the front doors, no longer breathing in the sticky sweet smell of the ice cream parlor. She had no intention of waiting for Stan; she didn't want him to know she cared, but there he was, sitting on a bench near the street. He grinned at her as she walked toward him, and in spite of herself she smiled shyly back at him.

"So, how far do you live from here?" he asked.

"It's a good thirty minute walk," Julianne admitted.

"Want me to just drive you? I brought my car," Stan said.

Alarm bells went off in Julianne's head. "No," she said, and he must have sensed the skepticism in her voice because he quickly said, "OK, OK, we'll walk. I'll just walk back here after."

The tone in which he answered assured Julianne that what she was doing was alright. Not like her mother or Amanda ever came to pick her up, she thought. She wondered if her mother even knew she had a job.

"So, Julie Martin," Stan began as they walked. "Tell me about yourself."

Julianne giggled. "What do you want to know?"

"Well, for starters, what's your family like?" Stan asked.

Julianne stiffened. She didn't want Stan to know anything about her family. So she just answered, "Well, it's pretty normal actually. I have two parents, and two sisters, Sarah and Mandy." It wasn't exactly a lie. "What about you?" she prodded. "You said you were visiting your aunt and uncle. You said you're from New Jersey?"

"Yup, New Jersey," Stan answered promptly. "I'm here kind of...taking some time away," he admitted slowly. "My parents are kind of going through a divorce. And I'm the only kid. They wanted me away for a little while, so they could figure things out on their own."

Julianne immediately felt sorry for him. Even though her family was ten times more fucked up than his, he sounded so genuinely upset that she couldn't help but feel bad. "I'm sorry," she said.

"It's cool," Stan said nonchalantly. "They've been fighting for so long that it's almost better this way."

"So how long are you here for?" she asked.

"Not really sure," Stan admitted. "I guess whenever my parents want me back, I'm going back. I'm here for at least the rest of the summer. If I like it, I might stay for the last year of high school, my aunt and uncle said I could stay as long as I wanted."

Julianne felt another pang of pity for Stan. He seemed like such a decent, yet unhappy guy all at the same time, it didn't seem fair.

"So what do your aunt and uncle do?" Julianne asked.

Stan hesitated, but for such a short moment that Julianne thought she might have imagined it. "My aunt stays at home," Stan said. "My uncle owns his own business. They don't have any kids." Julianne breathed a sigh of relief at this point; if his aunt and uncle didn't have children it was even more unlikely that they had heard about the Martell family and their tragedies.

"That's cool," Julianne said, "So you're kind of like their unofficial kid."

Stan laughed, and Julianne felt even more at ease. She found herself liking Stan more and more with every step they took, and she was filled with disappointment when her street sign came into view and she admitted, "This is my street."

Stan smiled at her and said, "I really want to see you again, Julie."

Julianne felt a warmth come over her that she had never experienced, and a happiness and excitement she had not known since her family fell apart. "I would like that too," she replied truthfully.

"Will you be taking a run tomorrow morning? I could meet you where we met today," Stan said.

Julianne nodded enthusiastically. "I'll meet you there tomorrow morning."

Stan reached out and gave her hand a little squeeze. "I'm really looking forward to it."

There was a fluttering in the pit of Julianne's stomach, and she had a sudden urge to lean forward and kiss Stan right on his perfect lips, but she refrained. "As am I," she said instead, smiling and turning around.

When Julianne walked into her house, Amanda was nowhere to be found and her mother was entertaining some strange man in the living room. "Julianne May, my love," Sandy called sweetly, "Come and meet Ron, my new friend."

Julianne looked at her mother's "new friend" with disgust. He was a rotund man who leered at Julianne with watery blue eyes and a ruddy face, and Julianne got the distinct impression that if he could have been sitting there on the couch with her instead of her mother, he would have been a much happier man.

"Pleasure to meet you," she said mechanically, then retreated to her room. She made sure to lock her door so that neither Ron nor her mother would be able to gain entrance, and still with the fluttery feeling in her stomach she changed into her pajamas, read a little bit of a book, and fell asleep.

Falling Apart

A s usual, the Sarah Jean debacle came back to Julianne in her dreams that night. Even though Julianne knew that they were flashbacks and mere memories, they felt all too real – and all too horrifying.

She remembered as though she were reliving it.

* * *

She was packing a bag for her and Amanda. She didn't even know what she was packing, or if they were her clothes or her sister's. She mechanically zipped up the duffel bag full of clothes, walked into her mother's room, and took out another bag and began to pack that as well.

Twenty minutes later, she put three bags in the front hallway and went back into the kitchen to see how Amanda was making out with her mother. Her father was on the phone, mumbling softly yet professionally to someone. Julianne guessed he was probably explaining the situation to someone at work.

Julianne glanced at her mother, who was now sitting in a chair while Amanda was rubbing her back. Sandy was still staring straight ahead at absolutely nothing.

Alan hung up the phone and turned around to face the members of his family. "OK, is everyone ready?" he asked softly.

"I packed everyone a bag and put them by the front door," Julianne said, her voice small. Her father walked past her and absentmindedly patted her on the head. "Good girl," he said. He looked at his wife sitting at the kitchen table, and with tears forming in the corners of his eyes he picked her up, cradling her in his arms like a baby. He leaned down and kissed her gently on the forehead, a tear falling on her cheek. Sandy was unresponsive. He then walked out of the kitchen toward the front door.

As soon as he was out of sight, Julianne and Amanda heard a choking sob, and then the wails of a devastated father mourning the loss of his baby girl. Julianne looked at her sister, whose china doll face suddenly fell, and she began weeping softly.

Everything was so surreal. Julianne walked over to Amanda and embraced her. As the sisters cried into each other's shoulders, they heard their father, still sobbing, open the front door and bring their mother out to the car. They were still holding each other and crying when he walked back in several minutes later, his eyes red-rimmed and puffy.

"Are you girls ready?"

Julianne and Amanda looked at their father, who suddenly seemed to have aged twenty years in the past hour. Alan stared back at them, at their two innocent faces, and something inside him knew at that moment he would never see all three of his daughters together again. Looking back, Julianne realized that this was the moment that Alan gave up on his family, even though he didn't run out on them until many months later.

Julianne could barely recall the ride to the airport, or the flight to Vermont. She remembered being greeted by police officers and detectives when they got off the plane, and her mother staring right through them like they weren't there, not even attempting to listen to them or answer any of their questions.

Alan Martell stoically began talking to them. They wanted to know if Sarah Jean had been dating anyone, when was the last time she had called home, if she had any enemies that they knew of at college. Alan answered the best he could; he said he had just spoken to Sarah Jean about forty-eight hours earlier, she said she was on her way out to a house party, and he couldn't think of anyone who would ever want to harm her. He admitted that he didn't know if she was dating anyone, and that's when they began questioning Julianne and Amanda.

Julianne was scared of the policemen. They were so cold and un-emotional as they probed her with questions about her sister. What were the names of her friends, did she like any boys, did she ever mention anything about the parties she went to. Julianne and Amanda didn't know anything about boys, or parties. If Sarah Jean was in-volved in any of that, she certainly didn't talk to her sisters about it.

When Julianne began crying, Alan Martell interfered. "OK, that's enough. Leave my daughters alone. Let me take my family to the hotel, please. We've had enough for one day."

Luckily, the policemen obliged, and Sandy, Julianne, and Amanda were whisked off in police cars to the hotel, where the girls helped their mother out of the car and into the elevator. Once upstairs, Amanda led Sandy to the large comfortable bed while Julianne began unpacking their bags. Julianne wished she could be more helpful with her mother, but Sandy was still on auto pilot – breathing, staring, blinking...but not speaking.

Alan had to go down to the police station so the police could show him the photos and evidence they had and talk to him about the details of the case. Alan never told the girls the actual details, but Julianne and Amanda read about them in all the papers for months afterward. *Last seen at eleven in the evening at a house party several blocks off campus, friends said she had a few drinks and was visibly intoxicated, met a guy at the party who no one seemed to recognize. Her friends, who also admitted to being intoxicated, said she was standing by the fireplace talking to a man, and then literally two minutes later she had disappeared.* The Martells learned that nearly everyone at the party had already been questioned, and not only did they not know the man she was speaking to, but no one even saw her leave. Her friends said this behavior was atypical for Sarah Jean; she wouldn't normally leave a party with a man, but by the time they went looking for her they realized she was already gone. Since their judgments were slightly impaired from the alcohol, they thought she may have just gone home and didn't pursue looking for her until no one heard from her the next day.

Julianne and Amanda put their mother to bed and watched television until they fell asleep. Julianne heard her father come in several hours later, and as he walked by the bed she could smell alcohol on him. She pretended to be asleep as he stood over the bed and looked at his family, crying softly. Julianne wanted to cry with him. She wanted to know where Sarah Jean was right at that very minute, and if she had any idea about what she was putting her family through.

The next morning dawned grey and damp, equaling the mood in the hotel room. The hotel telephone rang on the nightstand next to Sandy's head. Her eyes fluttered open and she watched it ring, but she made no motion to answer it. After five rings, Alan exhaled sharply, leaned over his wife and picked up the phone.

"Hello?" he said gruffly.

There was a long silence, and then he said softly, "OK, officer. I'll be down right away."

With an enormous sigh, Alan lifted himself out of bed and began getting dressed. Amanda sat up in bed and said, "Daddy, where are you going?"

"To the police station," Alan answered.

"Can we come?" Amanda asked.

A short pause, and then he uttered the words that Julianne would never forget as long as she lived. They came out of her father's mouth so terse, so matter-of-fact, and so definite that they haunted her dreams to this very day.

"I don't think that's a good idea, sweetheart. The police found a body, and they are ninety-nine percent sure it's Sarah Jean. They want me to go down to the morgue to identify her."

And with that he walked out of the hotel room, slamming the door without even looking at the girls or his wife.

Sandy Martell suddenly sprang to life.

"Sarah Jean? Did he say they found her? My baby? Oh, thank God, they found my baby girl!" she shrieked. Sandy suddenly leapt out of bed and began rifling through the duffel bags for her clothes.

"Mom," Amanda said, "Maybe you should let Daddy do it..."

"Nonsense!" Sandy said. "Sarah Jean will want to see her mother, of course."

Julianne looked at the swirly red and gold carpet below her feet. Her mother had completely lost it. All she heard was that Sarah Jean had been found. She must have blocked out the part that her father had said about Sarah Jean being a *body*. Which meant that if it was indeed her body, then she was no longer a somebody. Amanda and Julianne watched in horror as their mother smiled and danced around the room getting dressed in completely mismatched clothes. Julianne tried to protest, but Sandy Martell was so happy…it was the first time in two days the girls had seen some sign of life from their mother; they couldn't bear to tell her the truth and have her go back to the way she had been.

Before they could stop her, Sandy had dressed herself and run out the door, calling for her husband down the hotel corridor. Julianne prayed silently that her father had already left the hotel and was on his way to wherever he was going before her mother could catch up with him.

For the first time in hours, Julianne's prayers were answered. Her mother returned to the hotel room several minutes later, still animated and excited that her baby girl had been found.

"I'm just going to sit here and watch some television until your father brings her home," she said cheerfully, plunking down on the hotel bed. She looked at her two daughters who were watching her silently, with most of the color drained from their faces. "Why do you two look like the dog just died? Sarah Jean has been found! We're going to go home and be a family once again!"

Julianne tried to swallow, and suddenly found it very difficult to do so. Instead she began throwing up violently all over the bedspread. Sandy sprang up and held her hair back while she vomited, rubbing her back and saying, "It's alright, baby. I know it's been a rough few days."

Just as Julianne was done retching, Amanda burst into tears. "She isn't OK, mom! She's not OK! Nothing is ever going to be right again!"

Sandy had no idea that Amanda was talking about Sarah Jean. "Julianne is fine, sweetheart. Just a little nervous stomach. It happens to the best of us. It's been very stressful for all of us the past two days."

By this time Amanda was sobbing so hard her sentences were incomprehensible. In what would be one of Sandy's last motherly acts, she cleaned Julianne up and stripped the bed, and then went over and put her arms around a shrieking Amanda.

* * *

Julianne's dream faded away as she heard Amanda actually shrieking in her bedroom next to her. She looked at her clock, and when she saw that it read almost five in the morning, she figured Amanda had just gotten home and was talking to one of her degenerate friends on the telephone, being loud and disrespectful as usual. But several seconds later, she heard Amanda shriek again – and this time it sounded as if her voice was being muffled.

Julianne got up out of her bed and flung open her bedroom door. Amanda's bedroom door, right next to hers, was slightly ajar. Julianne peered in and was utterly horrified as she watched her mother's friend Rotund Ron, whose pants were lying on the floor, pin her sister down and try to tear her pants off. She burst in the room, her adrenaline pumping as she threw herself at Ron.

When Ron realized what was going on, he quickly jumped off the bed and put his pants back on. As he was buttoning them up, Julianne went over to Amanda who was crying softly on her bed. She looked at Julianne with puffy eyes and whispered softly, "Thank you," before dissolving into tears again. Anger welled up inside Julianne, and she turned on Ron.

"Get the hell out of here, you disgusting mother fucking bastard!" she screamed at him, not even caring if her mother heard her curse. "Get OUT!"

"You know what you people are?" Ron hissed at the sisters, sending small pieces of spittle into the air, "A house full of whores. You two are two little fucking whores, and your mother is the queen whore. Dirty sluts." And with that, he turned and walked out of Amanda's room.

Julianne didn't let out the breath she was holding in until she heard the front door slam. She turned to Amanda.

"Mandy...what happened?" she asked.

Amanda sniffled and chewed on her bottom lip. "I don't even know. I came home and they were sitting on the couch. It looked like they were both passed out. I came into my room and sat down at my desk chair, and the next thing I knew that disgusting pervert was pinning me down on my bed."

Julianne looked at her sister's attire. She hated to say that Amanda was asking for it, but with her ass hanging out of her super short denim miniskirt, her red bra pushing her breasts up, showing more cleavage than necessary, and her thick black eyeliner and bright red lipstick, Amanda did look like she should have been working on a corner. However, that did not give Ron the right to think he could touch her.

"I'm sorry, Mandy. I'm just glad I heard you," Julianne said. "I wonder what happened to Mom."

"What happens to her every night," Amanda spat bitterly. "She's fucking passed out on the couch. She has no idea. She'll probably blame me in the morning because he isn't here."

Julianne sighed, knowing that Amanda was right. Her mother was not going to be happy in the morning when she woke up and her "friend" was gone. And Julianne and Amanda doubted her mother would believe what had actually happened. Julianne didn't know what else to say or do about the troubles that seemed to keep following her family.

"I'm alright, Julianne," Amanda said, beginning to peel off her skintight clothing. "Go to bed. I'll see you in the morning."

What Happened To Daddy

J ulianne listlessly returned to her bed, too tired to argue with her
sister. She tossed and turned for two hours, which to her was
actually a nice change from the Sarah Jean nightmares that
constantly plagued her. At eight the next morning, she decided to go
for her morning run a little early. She didn't want to be anywhere
near her mother when Sandy woke up and realized that Ron had
walked out on her last night. She also didn't want to be anywhere
around Amanda when she woke up and completely ignored how
Julianne had saved her from getting raped just hours earlier.

Julianne tried on three different running outfits before settling on
a pair of black pants and a tight pink shirt. She wished her tiny
breasts filled out her sports bra a little more, but there was no time for
that. Last but not least, she put on just a tad of lip gloss and blush, just
enough to make it look like she wasn't trying. She gave herself one
last look in the mirror and thought she looked pretty cute for her first
unofficial "date" with Stan Douglas.

After she had been running for almost half an hour with no sign
of life in sight, Julianne was utterly thrilled to see Stan Douglas
walking toward her with the largest grin she had ever seen on a boy's

face. Julianne immediately tried to think of the last time someone was that genuinely happy to see her...and failed.

"Well, well, well, if it isn't Little Miss Ice Cream Scooper," Stan joked, and Julianne laughed. "Running again?"

"And what are you doing, *not* running again?" Julianne poked back at him, and once again was amazed at how easy teasing and flirting with him came to her.

"You're silly," he said, grinning again, and Julianne couldn't help but feel a little tug at her immature heartstrings as she smiled longingly back at him.

"So, when are we going to go on an official date?" Stan asked. Julianne was taken aback, and the look of shock on her face must have been obvious to Stan. He immediately added, "I mean, I like you Julie and I really would like to get to know you better, something other than running into you every morning." He gave a little half smile at his painful attempt at a pun. But his voice was so calm and genuine sounding that Julianne felt almost guilty for thinking that he was having impure thoughts.

"Aren't you, like, so much older than me though?" Julianne asked him. "Are you sure you want to date someone my age?"

"Oh please," Stan answered matter-of-factly. "I'm not that much older. You make me sound like an old man and I'm only seventeen. What are you, sixteen?"

"Fifteen, actually," Julianne answered quickly. She was starting to get a little nervous and she didn't know why. She had been a lot more comfortable around Stan when it was all nonsense and jokes.

Stan must have sensed her uneasiness, because he backed off.

"OK, Julie, well you have to continue your run, and I have to run a few errands for my aunt and uncle. Hope to see you around, though. Maybe you'll eventually change your mind about that date."

He gave her his signature grin and a wink and Julianne could feel her insides getting all warm again. She suddenly wished she weren't so shy – that she were as beautiful and confident as Sarah Jean, or at least as sexually sure as Amanda – but before she could channel either of her sisters, Stan was off and running.

Julianne's heart sank as she jogged back home. She figured she had completely ruined things with Stan, and he would never again seek her out while she was running or working. And she didn't even know where his aunt and uncle lived so she couldn't stop by his house. By the time she saw her street, she was even more depressed than she usually was upon re-entering her private hell.

Thankfully, Sandy was still fast asleep on the couch when Julianne quietly opened the door. It was only ten in the morning after all; Sandy wouldn't be up for at least another hour. Her prayers were answered further when she heard Amanda's soft snoring on her way back down the hall toward her room.

Closing her bedroom door and breathing a small sigh of relief, Julianne flipped on her small black and white television and found herself wondering where her father was at that very moment. Several seconds later, her favorite television show came on and she was lost in the world of "Family Ties" for the next thirty minutes.

Julianne got up as the end credits rolled and sat down at her desk. As she was checking her calendar to see what time she had to work later that day, she heard a newscast on the television behind her and her heart nearly stopped.

"Father of the missing Long Island beauty who was found dead at her college in Vermont one year ago, arrested last evening. Tune in tonight at five to find out why!"

Julianne could barely feel her head as she swirled around to look at the television just in time to see her father being pushed into a police car in handcuffs. Suddenly the next commercial came on and he was gone. He looked so thin and pale since the last time Julianne had seen him, which was well over a year ago. But there was no mistaking his face – it was definitely Alan Martell.

Julianne didn't know whether to scream or cry. She tried to open her mouth but it had suddenly become as dry as the desert. She heard a roaring sound in her ears, her legs gave way beneath her, and she was all of a sudden aware of her rear end hitting the floor with a loud thud. She sat there, rocking back and forth, waiting to see her father's face on the television again – but there was nothing. Julianne wondered if it had all just been a dream, but then Amanda came busting in the door, apparently irritated that Julianne's crashing to the ground had broken her slumber.

"What the hell, Julianne," Amanda blurted rudely, her eye makeup smeared all over her face.

Julianne turned toward her sister, her face scared and small.

"Daddy's on the news," was all she whispered. The color immediately drained from Amanda's face. "Fuck yourself, Julianne," she hissed, "You liar. Why would you say something like that?"

"I'm not lying," Julianne whispered. "Amanda, he was arrested."

"You're a fucking liar!" Amanda shrieked. "Daddy's gone! He's fucking gone, Julianne, he left us! As far as I'm concerned, he's fucking DEAD! DEAD, DO YOU HEAR ME?"

Julianne snapped out of it quickly when she realized that Amanda's shrieking was going to wake their mother, which was definitely something she did not want to happen. "Shut up, Amanda, you're going to wake Mommy," Julianne said.

"I don't give a shit," Amanda said, her voice still loud, but not as loud as it had just been. "I swear to God, Julianne, why would you lie like that? Why? When you know…what we…." Suddenly Amanda's voice broke and she began sniffling and sobbing and wailing.

"You know what we have gone through! What we've been going through! What we've all been dealing with!" Amanda cried.

Julianne leapt up and tried to console her sister, but was instantly annoyed that she had to be the one to do so. Although she so longed for bonding experiences with Amanda, this was not exactly what she had in mind. However, keeping Amanda quiet was her main focus at the moment, because she didn't want Sandy Martell to wake up and find out what was going on.

After her chance encounter with Stan, Julianne didn't really think she was going to get lucky two times in one day. Before she could subside Amanda's wails, she heard Sandy's footsteps thumping down the hallway.

"Amandaaaaaa!" Sandy yelled in her throaty voice. "What the hell is the problem?"

Amanda heard Sandy's voice and ceased her sobbing immediately. "Shit," she cursed, and wiped her nose. "I told you," Julianne said stonily. Their mother thumped right by Julianne's room and they heard her fling open Amanda's door.

"Where are you?" Sandy hissed.

Julianne had an idea. She hoped Amanda would go along with it. "Amanda," she whispered, knowing that Sandy was moments away from stomping into her room and finding them slumped on the floor, "Get into my bed and pretend we're watching television." Julianne picked herself up and threw herself into bed, patting the covers. "Hurry!"

It took Amanda longer than it should have, but she finally figured out what Julianne was asking her to do. She knew she didn't want to deal with the hung-over wrath of Sandy either, because she hopped up and sat down on the bed next to Julianne. Just then, Sandy threw open the bedroom door.

"What is going on in here?" Sandy asked, one eye slanted.

"Nothing," Julianne said quickly, "We were just watching television."

"What's with all the God damn screaming?"

"Television," Amanda said rapidly, catching on to Julianne's game, "We probably just had the television on too loud."

Sandy looked skeptical but the girls could tell she was in no mood to argue. "Fine," she said warily. "Keep it down, my head hurts."

Julianne rolled her eyes as her mother lumbered back down the hallway calling out, "Ron? Where are you, honey?"

Amanda's face became stony again when she heard her mother calling out for the man who had just assaulted her hours earlier. At the mention of his name, she transformed back into mean Amanda and swiftly picked herself up off the bed, heading for Julianne's door.

"I don't care what kind of shit you've got going on, Julianne," she said, "But in case you haven't noticed, we're all fucked up around here. You going and making up stories about seeing Daddy on television isn't helping shit." And before Julianne could even protest, she was gone.

Julianne sank back into her bed. She had to go to work in two hours and she could barely muster the strength to pick her head up off the pillow. She tried to remember what the newscaster had said about her father but all she could picture was his face – sallow and sunken and sad.

She wished there were someone she could ask to watch the five o'clock news for her, but she didn't have any close friends and she surely couldn't ask her mother or sister to do it. She hoped that they wouldn't watch the news, but then she realized that she didn't think either one of them had turned on the TV in months so she probably didn't have to worry. Julianne frantically tried to think of another way that she could find out the information she was looking for.

Julianne had an uneventful night at work. As she thought about the news clip she had seen earlier, she hoped that the newscast wouldn't show pictures of their family. Julianne felt a sudden surge of anger toward her father. Hadn't they all suffered enough? What was he doing putting himself in the public eye again? Sarah Jean's disappearance had been the main story in the area for months, and they had to endure reporters hovering and photographers snapping pictures of the remaining Martells even as they left their house in the morning for school or work. Julianne didn't want anything like that to ever happen to her again – it was as if she had suddenly become a local celebrity, with the media covering her every move, and she hated it. Stan's face also flashed into her head, and she realized she didn't want to ruin whatever chance she might have had left with him.

Work dragged on for Julianne. Katherine chattered incessantly about how far she had let her boyfriend go the night before, and Julianne feigned interest. She desperately hoped that Stan would walk through the door, but there was no sign of him all night.

When she got home from working at Seth's that evening, Sandy and Amanda were not there. Julianne breathed a sigh of relief and went to her room to get ready for bed. She was hoping that her father's story would be on the eleven o'clock news, so she switched on the tiny television set that sat on her bureau. She changed into her pajamas and patiently sat on her bed waiting to see that recognizable yet unfamiliar face flash on the TV screen. But there was nothing at all on her father or any other crimes in the area for that matter.

The next morning, Julianne purchased a newspaper on the way back from her morning run. When she got home she ran to her room, locked the door, and immediately tore through the paper looking for anything relating to what she had seen on the news the day before

Just when she was about to check herself into an insane asylum thinking she had imagined the broadcast, there it was – on the second-to-last page of the paper, a headline so small and insignificant and so low to the bottom of the page that only people who *really* scoured the newspaper cover-to-cover would see it – exactly the information that Julianne was looking for:

FATHER OF SLAIN LOCAL BEAUTY ARRESTED FOR ARMED ROBBERY, the headline read. Julianne devoured the article, horrified.

Alan Martell, whose daughter Sarah Jean Martell's disappearance and homicide last year remains unsolved, was arrested yesterday when local authorities were alerted by an anonymous caller about a masked man breaking into a small boutique store on Kaplan Street in Simsbury, NY.

When police arrived on the scene, they found Martell, 41, behind the store counter huddled in a ball and shaking. He had not even attempted to break into the register, but was armed with a semi-automatic weapon. After his apprehension, toxicology results indicated that Mr. Martell had undisclosed amounts of heroin in his bloodstream. He was arrested immediately and placed in jail.

Martell's family made headlines last year when his eldest daughter, Sarah Jean, 19, disappeared from college in Vermont and was later found dead. The police have tried unsuccessfully to apprehend her killer, but to this date no arrest has been made and the case remains open and unsolved.

Alan Martell has no known family; he has been estranged from his wife and daughters since Sarah Jean's death last year. He has been living in a small apartment in Taxston and was on the verge of eviction for past due rent.

Julianne was horrified. She put the paper down as tears poured out over her cheeks. This was her family legacy. This was the history she would share with her future husband, and children, and grandchildren. She could just hear herself telling the story now – "After your Aunt Sarah Jean was killed, Grandma became an alcoholic, Grandpa became a heroin addict –Oh! And Aunt Amanda became a slut."

It was then that Julianne decided that she had had enough with her family and her life, and she vowed to herself that she would get away from Carrollton, Long Island as soon as she possibly could. She was intelligent enough to know that she couldn't run away with the scant amount of money she had saved up; she didn't even have enough to rent her own place. Furthermore, she was not old enough to sign any kind of lease, and she didn't know anyone old enough that would sign for her. She knew that her only chance was to find someone to move away with. Since she didn't have any friends, she figured her only chance was to find a boy who would fall in love with her and whisk her away from her life, which quite honestly didn't amount to much. Boys fell in love with Amanda and Sarah Jean all the time, and she was a Martell after all, so how hard could it be?

Family Lies

The next day when she was on her run, she spotted Stan Douglas a couple hundred yards ahead of her, heading in her direction. Julianne mustered up all the courage that she possibly could, combined it with her insatiable desire for freedom from her family, put a smile on her face and jogged right up to him.

"Well, hello, there," Stan said brightly. Julianne cocked her head to the side and smiled slyly at Stan, trying to imitate the smile she had seen Amanda give so many of her male friends.

"What's up, Mr. Douglas?" she asked coyly. Stan must have sensed a change in Julianne's demeanor because he responded with immediate flirtation. "Oh, not much Miss Martin. Interested in maybe going on a date later? I'll even come over and introduce myself to your parents first if you want."

Julianne was instantly nervous. "Oh, that's not, um, really...uh...necessary," she stammered. "They're ah...on vacation. They'll be gone for the next two weeks."

Stan's eyes lit up. "Oh really? Who are you staying home with?"

"My sisters," Julianne responded nonchalantly.

"How old are they?" Stan asked.

"Mandy is seventeen and Sarah is twenty."

"Gotcha. So you're the baby?" Stan teased.

"Technically speaking," Julianne said with a wink. "But I'm not that young."

Stan threw his head back and laughed. "Well I'm not sure what made you change your attitude toward me, but I'm sure glad you did. I kind of figured after the last time I saw you that I made you nervous and you would never hang out with me again."

Julianne channeled every ounce of Amanda's promiscuity and said, "I'd love to do more than hang out with you."

Stan's eyes widened for a minute and Julianne thought she saw a hint of nervousness from him now, but it was so quick she figured she had imagined it. "Alright then," he said, "Can I pick you up tonight at seven?"

"How about I meet you at the ice cream parlor?" Julianne replied, thinking quickly. "I have to work anyway, and I can just change and meet you after." It was a total lie – she didn't have to work, but the last thing she needed was Stan Douglas ringing her doorbell and her mother answering it reeking of vodka.

Stan nodded his approval. "Well, I will let you get back to your run, Julie, and I can't tell you how much I look forward to seeing you later tonight."

Julianne smiled, and found herself actually excited as she turned around and jogged off. She wanted so badly to turn around and see if Stan was looking at her but she didn't want to risk catching his eyes again. Her very first date! Julianne felt a wave of sadness wash over her; she wished she could share this with Amanda and Sarah Jean, or even her mother, but then she shook off the wishful thinking and got back into her new Julianne mindset.

The rest of the day practically flew by. At half past five, Julianne got in the shower and got ready for her date, appreciative that her mother and Amanda didn't ask where she was going. She left her house a half an hour before she was to meet Stan, and got to the ice cream parlor a little before seven, which was her plan, so Stan would think that she had just gotten off work.

She saw him striding down the street just a few minutes after seven, and her heart and mind began to race. What was she doing? Was this right? Before any more questions arose, Julianne pushed them all out of her mind and strode over to him.

"You look nice," Stan commented. Julianne blushed and looked down at the ground. "Thank you," she replied.

"So, I was thinking maybe we could go to a movie and then get a shake or something?" Stan said. "You know, just a typical first date. I don't want you to feel uncomfortable or anything."

Julianne was pleased that he was acting like a gentleman. Even though this was the new Julianne and she was determined to do whatever it took to get a man to fall in love with her and get her out of Carrollton, it was easier when the man was not acting like a jerk.

"Sounds great," Julianne smiled, and Stan took her hand in his and led her in the direction of the movie theater.

The date was an absolute success – Julianne couldn't remember the last time that she had smiled or laughed so much. She so looked forward to spending more time with Stan in the coming weeks. He was easy to talk to, and even though he asked questions about her family that she didn't want to answer, when he sensed that she was uncomfortable talking about it he steered the conversation in a completely different direction. He held doors for her, paid for everything, and put his arm around her shoulder in just the right spot while they were watching the movie.

Julianne was disappointed when her time with Stan had to end. She didn't want to leave him….he made her feel so safe, so protected – something she had not felt in a very long time. He walked her to the end of her street and leaned his face down to hers and gently kissed her on the lips. As he pulled away, Julianne leaned in for more, and he obliged. They made out on the corner of Senderfill Street for nearly thirty minutes, and even though pulling away from Stan and going back to her house was heart wrenching, it left Julianne with a thirst only he could quench.

Julianne was in a state of euphoria when she walked back into her house. She barely noticed her mother sitting on the couch with yet another man, she didn't care that Amanda was nowhere to be found; she just walked right into her room and fell back onto her bed, hugging herself and smiling. Julianne knew she was in love, and she hoped that Stan felt the same way. Julianne fell asleep with no problems that night – she didn't wait up for Amanda, and she didn't have the recurring Sarah Jean nightmare. It was the best night's sleep she had had in a very long time, and she had Stan Douglas to thank for it.

Stan and Julianne spent almost every evening together for the next few weeks, and before long he invited her back to his house to meet his aunt and uncle. Julianne liked Stan's Aunt Debbie, and his Uncle Charlie was definitely a character. She wanted to know what kind of business a person ran that required them to run around the house all day in a track suit talking in hushed tones on the telephone, but she didn't dare ask Stan. She figured it would probably come out in time.

Julianne started spending the night at Stan's house. Aunt Debbie consented to the sleepovers as long as Stan's bedroom door stayed open. And, even though Stan wanted to, they had not had sex yet. Julianne found herself staying there more and more, mainly to avoid the horrific scene at her own house. Since neither her mother nor Amanda ever asked where she was, she didn't feel the need to go home.

When Stan and Julianne had been dating for about three months, Stan demanded to meet Julianne's family. It was their first real fight, and it went on for days. Up until then, Julianne had successfully made excuses for why Stan couldn't come over to meet her family – her dad was away on business, her mom was sick, her sisters weren't home – but now Stan was not taking the excuses anymore and began to get angry.

"You know my family, Julie," Stan said. "My aunt and uncle ask you to eat dinner and stay over all the time, the least you could do is introduce me to your parents. Do they even exist? Why can't I meet them? Are you ashamed of me or something?"

The last question stung Julianne even more than the others. She would never want Stan to think that she was ashamed of him— she loved him dearly. Julianne closed her eyes and breathed out slowly, trying to conjure up yet another lie, but she couldn't. She realized that she was sick of lying, especially to Stan. She thought that he would probably hate her forever because she had been lying to him for months, but she needed to share her trauma with someone, anyone, and she knew Stan would at least hear her out and wouldn't hate her....because he loved her too much.

"You're going to want to sit down for this, Stan," Julianne whispered.

"Jule? What's the matter?" Stan's brow furrowed, but he sat down and put his hand gently on Julianne's knee.

"I haven't exactly been…honest. With you, I mean," Julianne began. "But it's for good reason, and I really want you to hear me out, please?"

Stan's expression hardened when he heard that he had been duped, but as he looked into Julianne's pretty blue eyes he seemed to sense there was something that he needed to hear, so he nodded for her to continue.

"First of all, my name is Julianne Martell, not Julie Martin. I used to have two sisters, and a mother and father, but last year my oldest sister Sarah Jean was killed and my father went crazy and left us."

Julianne could not even look at Stan; she was terrified of how he was going to react. She couldn't bear to lose him, and she feared that after she revealed her secret he would be gone. Julianne kept her eyes on the carpet and could feel something start to rise up in her throat. Slamming her lips shut, she gulped several times but still did not look up. The feeling subsided. She almost didn't want to continue, but Stan squeezed her arm and so she kept going.

"As if that weren't bad enough, since my father left, my sister Amanda goes with random boys and does who knows what with them, and my mother drinks…all the time–it's been—really—um, hard—" Julianne's voice trailed off and her shoulders started to sink.

She felt Stan's finger under her chin lifting her face up to look him in the eyes. "Why did you lie to me about your name?" he asked tenderly, but already knowing the answer.

"Because everyone around here knows my family. We're tainted. No one wants to be friends with us or date us or anything – we're all like damaged goods." At this, Julianne broke into tears. "I was scared that you would tell your aunt and uncle my name and they wouldn't let you near me because I'm from the crazy family in town..."

Before Julianne could continue, Stan pulled her close and hugged her tightly. "Listen to me, Jule. I love you no matter what your name is, who your family is, or where they are right now. Yes, I am a bit irritated that I've been dating Julie Martin for the past three months when in fact your name is Julianne Martell, but really...I'm in love with *you* and not anyone else," Stan sighed deeply and continued, "I'm sorry that things haven't been easy for you, but I promise from here on out that I am going to do everything I can to make the rest of your life better than it's been for you."

The fact that he was being so nice about it only made Julianne sob harder. *She was lucky to have found Stan,* she thought. When she calmed down, he asked her several more questions about her past, because he was curious, but he chose his words carefully. At the end of the conversation, he said, "Julianne, I would still like to meet your family, but I understand if you don't want me to. I will wait until you're ready." Julianne kissed him, her lips salty from tears, and snuggled close to him.

Julianne slept fitfully that night, even though Stan wrapped his strong arms around her and didn't let go once. She was trying to figure out the easiest way to introduce him to her mother and Amanda and her brain began to hurt after several hours because it just didn't seem that there was an easy way. Her mother would probably be drunk; Amanda would throw herself at him shamelessly. The last thing she wanted to do was to ruin things with Stan, but he seemed set on meeting them no matter what.

A Brief Moment of Normalcy

The next day, Julianne went home after her afternoon shift at the ice cream parlor, ready to attempt the first normal conversation she would have with her mother in over a year. She practiced it over and over while she was at work, and she walked into the house shortly after three in the afternoon to find Sandy sitting on the couch with a bottle of vodka on the coffee table in front of her and a glass tumbler in her hand, eyes fixed on the television.

Julianne took a glance at the bottle and thought that she might have half a fighting chance of having a reasonable chat with Sandy because she was apparently only on her first drink. She took a deep breath and walked over to her mom and sat down quietly on the couch next to her.

Sandy lazily turned her head toward her youngest daughter. "Yes, Miss Julianne?" she said evenly. "Can I help you?"

"Mom, can I talk to you about something?" Julianne asked timidly.

Sandy's eyes hardened with pain. Julianne was scared for a moment, but realized quickly that Sandy probably wanted to have an ordinary mother-daughter conversation just as badly as she did. Julianne remembered how Sarah Jean and her mother used to talk for hours and hours, laughing and brushing each other's hair as they talked about everything from boys to school to music. Sometimes Julianne forgot that she was not the only family member that lost a best friend when Sarah Jean died.

"Of course you can, Julie Bean," Sandy said softly.

Julianne's eyes filled with tears and she had to bite her lower lip to keep them from spilling over. Her mom hadn't called her Julie Bean since before…

But there was no time to think about that now. Julianne pictured Stan's face in her mind and pushed forward.

"Well, mom, I met a boy," Julianne began. Sandy's expression softened and her lips curved into a bit of what Julianne thought might be a smile, so she felt comfortable continuing. "His name is Stan Douglas, and he lives in the next town over. He's seventeen—"

"Ah, older man, huh?" Sandy interrupted. "Good for you, darling."

"Yes, he's really wonderful to me, Mom. We've been dating for a little over three months now, and I've met his aunt and uncle, who he lives with, and I was wondering if…if…maybe…I could bring him over here so you could meet him?"

Julianne looked down and tried not to flinch as she waited for her mother's caustic response. But she got the shock of her life when she heard Sandy say, "That would be very nice, Julianne. I'm sure he's a lovely young man and I would like very much to meet him if he is making you happy."

"Really?"

Sandy nodded, but aside from the smile Julianne thought she saw a few moments ago her face stayed basically expressionless.

"Is that where you've been staying when you don't come home at night?" Sandy queried.

Julianne nodded. "I didn't think you noticed...I'm sorry I didn't ask..."

"It's alright. I know I haven't..." Sandy started, but shook her head, not wanting to continue. "As long as you are safe."

"Thanks, mom. I'll probably have him come by tonight." Julianne gave a sidelong glance at the vodka bottle sitting in front of her mother, and then looked at the ground. "What time should I tell him?"

Sandy put down her glass of vodka, the ice making a lonely clinking sound as it hit the wooden table. "I'll get in the shower right now. Why not ask him to come over at about six?"

Julianne couldn't believe how smoothly this was going. She hadn't even had to say half of what she had practiced all day at work. She reached out and took the bottle of vodka and half full glass and said, "Want me to put these away?"

Suddenly the old Sandy was back. "No," she said, pulling the glass out of Julianne's hand. She got up and walked down the hallway into her bedroom, and Julianne heard her start the shower.

Oh well, Julianne thought, *can't win 'em all.* She just hoped she could get Stan to come over before her mother made it halfway through that bottle.

Undaunted, Julianne went into the kitchen and picked up the telephone to dial Stan's number. He was expecting her call; he answered after the first ring.

"So, I talked to my mom, and she wants to meet you tonight," Julianne said.

"Really? That's great. What time do you want me to come over?"

"How about six?"

"Six is perfect. I will see you then. Should I bring anything?"

Julianne inhaled sharply. "Just your sense of humor and an open mind. And I apologize ahead of time if anything should…uh, happen."

Stan shushed her. "I told you, Julianne. I love you. Everyone's family has their skeletons. Even mine."

His last sentence piqued her curiosity. "Yours? What do you mean?"

"We'll talk about it later. There's something that I need to tell you about my aunt and uncle."

Julianne didn't reply. Stan must have sensed that he scared her a little, because he said, "It doesn't involve me or you and it's nothing really terrible. Just not something I like broadcasting. But, since I love you, I think it's something you should know."

Although she was still curious, Julianne let it rest for the moment. A part of her was even a bit happy that Stan's family had secrets just like her own. She said goodbye to Stan and went into her room to change before he came over.

Julianne realized she hadn't seen or heard Amanda since she had been home, and her mother hadn't mentioned if she was there or not. Julianne cautiously tiptoed towards Amanda's door and pushed it open ever so slightly. She did not see Amanda sleeping on her bed, so she pushed it open further and listened. Nothing.

Maybe I'll get lucky and she just won't come home, Julianne thought. Amanda's state of mind was more of a gamble than her mother's most of the time – while Sandy only had a thing for the drink, one never knew what substance Amanda would be on when she walked into the house.

The doorbell rang at five minutes to six, and Julianne happily pranced toward the foyer to open it and welcome her boyfriend to her home. Sandy ambled out of her bedroom, looking more put together than she had in months, but Julianne recognized the glassiness of her eyes and wondered how much more of that bottle she had drunk in the past two hours.

Julianne opened the door and after taking a glance at Stan, she took a moment to catch her breath. With his caring brown eyes staring down at her from a good seven inches higher than her own five and a half feet, he was simply a vision of perfection to her. She took in every inch of him, silently wondering for the umpteenth time how she had gotten so lucky.

Stan stepped inside and leaned down to kiss Julianne on the cheek. He looked around the foyer, at the pictures hanging on the wall that desperately needed dusting, and smiled as he took her hand. She grabbed his in return but didn't move, and leaned forward to kiss him on the cheek. He looked at her expectantly.

"Well, what are we waiting for?" he asked, a bit nervously. "Let's do this."

Julianne didn't blame him. If she were meeting her family for the first time, she'd be nervous too. She led him into the kitchen where she had heard her mother opening and shutting cabinets a few moments earlier.

"Mom," Julianne said, "This is Stan Douglas, my boyfriend. Stan, my mother Sandy Martell."

Sandy shook Stan's hand and said, "Pleasure to meet you, Stan. Julianne has said some lovely things about you."

If Stan had picked up on her slight slur and the hint of vodka on her breath, he didn't flinch. "She has said lovely things about you as well, Mrs. Martell. I'm so glad to finally meet you."

Julianne almost laughed out loud. Trying to contain herself, she said, "Stan, would you like a cup of tea?"

"Yes, I was just about to put the kettle on," Sandy said, going over to the stove and filling the teakettle with tap water. Julianne helped her mother set the table with three teacups and saucers, and she got the milk out of the refrigerator as Sandy fumbled in the cabinet for sugar.

The scene was surreal. The sheer commonness of the situation–a mother meeting a boyfriend, the three of them sitting down for tea, it was all something she had never experienced. Every day in her house was a crap shoot; she never knew what to expect when she opened her eyes in the morning. Normalcy had long since become unusual in the Martell household.

Sandy poured the hot water into each of the cups on the table and then returned the kettle to the stove. On her way to sit back down at the table, she nonchalantly picked up the half-drank vodka bottle and set it down next to her teacup and saucer. "So where are you from?" she asked Stan.

"New Jersey," Stan answered. "Hackettstown, out in west Jersey closer to Pennyslvania."

"Oh, I've heard it's nice out that way," Sandy said absentmindedly, picking up the bottle and pouring a shot of vodka into her tea. Julianne shot a look at Stan, who was stirring his tea and didn't seem to notice.

"Yes, it is. I'm out here visiting my aunt and uncle for the summer. My parents are going through a bit of a rough time..." Stan's voice trailed off.

"That happens with parents," Sandy said bitterly. "You think you love someone and then BAM, your daughter dies and your husband leaves you. Case closed."

Stan looked shocked only for a moment, but continued along with the conversation not skipping a beat. "Yeah, it's rough."

Julianne was seconds away from breaking into a cold sweat. She tried to steer the conversation away from family and said, "So, Stan, why don't you tell my mom what you're planning on majoring in at college?"

Before Stan had a chance to answer, Sandy interrupted. "College is almost as rough as marriage. Letting your kids go is one of the stupidest decisions you could ever make. Lucky for me Amanda and Julianne aren't going to college."

Tears stung Julianne's eyes and threatened to pour out, and she had to look away when Stan looked at her. Julianne longed to go to college, and she knew she wouldn't make the same idiotic decisions that Sarah Jean had. But apparently her mother had other plans...Plans that she had not chosen to share with Julianne until this moment in time.

"College is a good place for learning, both scholarly lessons and life lessons," Stan replied nonchalantly back to Sandy. Sandy looked up from her tea and stared at Stan. Julianne was scared for a minute that it was going to be another outburst, but her mother just said, "Yes, lessons."

The front door slammed and Julianne cringed in horror as Amanda walked into the kitchen. Thankfully she wasn't drunk, but she was clad in her slut attire and she looked from Sandy to Julianne to Stan before blurting out, "Who the hell are you?"

Sandy stood up and put her arm around Amanda and said, "Mandy, this is Julianne's boyfriend, Sam."

"Stan," Julianne corrected.

"Right, Stan," Sandy said. "Why don't you sit down and have a cup of tea with us?"

Amanda snorted and cocked her lips in a crooked smile. "Thanks but no thanks. I have more important things to do." She ducked out of the kitchen, and Julianne was too embarrassed to say anything. Two seconds later she poked her head back into the door frame and said, "But hey, Stan, when you're done with my sister have her give you my number. We should go out sometime." And with a wink and a smirk she was gone again.

Julianne was horrified. Stan looked at Julianne and smiled, and put his hand on her leg. Julianne wanted this "meeting" to be over as soon as possible. She wanted to get Stan out of her house and away from her mother and sister before they did anything else to strip her of her last remaining shreds of dignity.

The next half hour passed rather uneventfully, aside from several of Sandy's unnecessary slurs, and the fact that she kept pouring vodka into her tea. Stan handled all of her advances with poise and grace. With every calm response he directed at Sandy, Julianne fell deeper in love with him, and she knew that Stan was the man she was destined to spend the rest of her life with. She imagined him whisking her off to Hackettstown, New Jersey and living out the rest of her life with him in happiness...without her mother or sister around to ruin it.

When Stan announced that he and Julianne would have to leave in order to get to their movie on time, Julianne thought that she would get down on her knees and thank him for all eternity...because she knew they weren't even going to a movie.

Stan embraced her mother and gave her a kiss on the cheek before he left, and when he walked out the door Sandy put a hand on Julianne's shoulder and said genuinely, "I like him, Julianne. Don't mess it up!"

Julianne smiled at her and gave her mom a big hug, something she hadn't done in months. To Julianne's utter shock and surprise, Sandy squeezed her back. "I love you, Julie Bean," she said.

The tears threatened to spill down Julianne's face, but she held them back. Who knew that doing something so simple as dating a boy would get her mother back to semi-normal? If she had known it, she would have found a boyfriend long ago.

Stan grabbed Julianne's hand on their walk down the driveway and said, "Julianne, listen. I know that you probably want to apologize, or explain, or give me some excuse, but you don't have to. Your mom and sister are great. And given the circumstances, the fact that they are still functioning...well, it's sort of...amazing. I feel really bad for you guys."

Julianne couldn't help herself anymore. She didn't want Stan's pity. The tears that had been threatening to spill over all night finally found their way down her pale cheeks. "Stan, I— "

"No," he said, putting a finger over Julianne's lips. "I love you, so I have to love your family. End of story."

Julianne stopped and threw her arms around him and sobbed into his chest. "Thank you," was all she could muster between sobs.

When she stopped crying and had disentangled herself from Stan, he said, "Julie, remember how I told you earlier I had something to tell you about my Uncle Charlie and Aunt Debbie?"

Julianne nodded. She could have never expected the sentence that followed. It almost made her wonder why she was so ashamed of her own family.

"Uncle Charlie owns a...um, a...sort of...prostitution ring," Stan hesitated and stuttered at first, but ultimately said it matter-of-factly. He didn't beat around the bush or anything. He just put it out there, as simply as if he would have said, "My eyes are blue".

"A—what?" Julianne stammered, unsure of what to say or how to take it.

"Look, it's not really a bad thing. All of his girls are registered, they all do it because they want to, and they make a ton of money. And in return, Uncle Charlie makes a ton of money. Which is why Aunt Debbie doesn't have to work," Stan added as an afterthought.

"But...what do...I mean, how...where...registered?" Julianne didn't know which question to ask first.

"I'm really not sure of all the logistics," Stan explained. "All I know is that girls look Uncle Charlie up and ask him to be their boss. Then he finds them men who want to sleep with them, and they pay the girls lots of money. They get a percentage of it but Uncle Charlie gets most of it. It's really a legit business actually. Uncle Charlie tells me that it's been going on for hundreds of years and it's the oldest profession in the world."

"But...is it legal?"

"I've never really asked, but I'm sure it is...I mean even if it's not, it isn't like it's really illegal. Uncle Charlie wouldn't do anything against the law, and he has been doing this as long as I can remember," Stan said. "I mean, he says it's like kind of on the line between legal and illegal. But it's also one of those things that we don't really tell other people. Just because...well...Uncle Charlie says there are lots of groups out there nowadays that disagree with paying for sex, so he doesn't want to get shut down."

"Why are you telling me this?" Julianne asked.

"Well," Stan began, choosing his words carefully, "You introduced me to some of your family secrets tonight, so I felt like I should share some of mine."

Julianne kind of wished he hadn't, but there was nothing she could do now. The proverbial cat was out of the bag. "So...should I be scared of him?" she asked.

"No of course not!" Stan assured. "He's still the same Uncle Charlie. He just...happens to manage girls who have sex for money."

Julianne was horrified, but curious at the same time. "How much money?"

Stan shrugged. "Uncle Charlie said his top girl makes almost a thousand dollars a week."

Julianne nearly fell over. A thousand dollars a week! She had been saving up her ice cream money for nearly six months and had just a little more than four hundred dollars. If she could make even four hundred dollars a week she would be out of Carrollton in less than a year. That was for sure.

"How old are the girls?" Julianne asked.

Stan continued answering Julianne's questions, unaware of what she was getting at. "Oh, there's a big range...I think the oldest one is in her thirties and the youngest one is sixteen or so."

"Well that is...interesting," Julianne said, for lack of a better word.

"You don't think less of Uncle Charlie...or me?" Stan asked, searching Julianne's face.

"Of course not," Julianne said. "People have to work for a living. You do what you gotta do. As long as it isn't illegal and he isn't getting in trouble for it, what do I care?"

Stan smiled. "This is why I love you, Julianne Martell. You're the most understanding person in the entire world."

Julianne squeezed his hand as they turned down his street and headed toward his house. Even though she pretended that the conversation was over, she knew she had many more questions about Uncle Charlie and his job. Stan turned the conversation over to the fact that he had convinced his parents to let him stay at Uncle Charlie and Aunt Debbie's house for his senior year of high school, and Julianne was elated. School was starting in just a few weeks, and she thought maybe, just maybe, she would earn a little more respect from her peers having an older boyfriend.

Goodbye Sarah Jean

J ulianne's sophomore year of high school had been less than
pleasant. Everyone knew about Sarah Jean's disappearance and
how her father had left. Then once Amanda started hanging out
with the bad crowd and sleeping around, Julianne's friends seemed
even more disinterested in her. She later learned through gossip that
her friends' parents were saying the Martell sisters were bad news,
and they were under strict orders to stay away. People only bothered
talking to her at school when they were telling her what slutty thing
her sister had done the weekend before. The fact that Stan would now
be her ally at school gave her hope for a normal school year. Besides,
she kept telling herself, he had skeletons just like she did. They were
two people with two whacked out families; they were clearly destined
for each other.

For the next couple of weeks before school started, every time
Julianne was at Stan's house she would watch Uncle Charlie. Now
that she knew what kind of profession he was running, his conversations made a little more sense. "Hi Mort. Janice, twenty-two, nine
tonight, one hundred and fifty dollars," he would say quickly over the
phone. And then he would hang up. Julianne was fascinated. Now

she understood that twenty-two year old Janice was meeting Mort at nine that evening and she would be getting a hundred and fifty dollars to have sex with him. The only thing she wondered was how much of that hundred and fifty Janice would get to keep. The amount of money involved in this business captivated her, and every time she would put her twenty or thirty dollars into the jar under her bed every week, she felt that there was more that she could be doing to earn the money to move away.

When school started, Julianne couldn't work at the ice cream parlor as much, especially since she wanted to spend time with Stan at night. So her hours were cut down to two nights a week and one day on the weekends. This had her putting only ten to fifteen dollars away per week, and she knew that this was just not going to cut it. Most of the time when she and Stan went out to dinner or a movie or ice cream, he paid, but sometimes she would, because she felt bad that he was always paying.

In October, Stan began applying to colleges. Most of them were in New Jersey, and this left Julianne wondering where she fit into Stan's plans. "Jule, you have to finish high school," he would say. "But we'll see each other every weekend, I promise. Aunt Debbie and Uncle Charlie said I can come here every weekend and stay at their place, and you can stay with me." This made Julianne somewhat depressed, because that would mean that she had to stay at her own house at least five nights a week. And she wasn't sure if she could handle that.

"What if I transferred to high school in New Jersey, near where you go to school?" she asked.

"I just don't know if that's possible," Stan sighed. "I would love it, but….I think you have to declare residency in a town in order to go to high school there, and you can't declare residency at my college dorm room...."

Julianne's face fell. Stan put his finger under her chin. "Look, Jule, this is just a small obstacle in what is going to be the rest of our lives. We both need to go to college so we can get good jobs, and you have to graduate high school to go to college. When you graduate, you'll apply to my college. So that way it will only be one year that we're apart."

Julianne looked up at him, her face small and scared. "But I..." she began, and he stopped her.

"I know, Julianne. I know you don't want to be there. I wish there was something I could do to change things but...I don't think there is."

Even though Stan would be leaving her next fall, Julianne was still thankful that she had found someone who really understood her and was sympathetic to her dreadful home situation. The nights that she had to sleep at home were usually always the same scenario – her mother bringing random men home, passing out drunk on the couch, and Amanda slutting it up and coming home at five in the morning. She sometimes felt small pangs of sympathy for Amanda, and hoped that she was using condoms when she had casual sex, as well as locking her bedroom door to protect herself from more potential bad situations with Sandy's boyfriends. Her encounters with her mother and sister had been limited due to the minute amount of time that she spent at home, and for that she was thankful. Her mother actually asked her every now and then, how Stan was doing, and then she would comment about "what a nice boy" he was.

School was, as Julianne had predicted, more bearable because of Stan. She now had someone to walk from class to class with, eat lunch with, and protect her from the judgmental stares of her classmates as she walked through the halls. In fact, the only stares she was getting now were those of envy – because she was dating one of the hottest senior boys at her high school.

And Stan, to his credit, only had eyes for Julianne. Girls would giggle and coo at him, and try to talk to him, and he would wave them away without even a second look. He focused on his studies and Julianne, and nothing else.

As the days went by, Julianne thanked God each and every night for sending her Stan, who she considered her angel. The man who had cared enough to get to know her, and who loved her despite her sordid past. The man who took her away from the nightmare of her daily life. The man who wanted to spend the rest of his life with her.

For Christmas, Julianne got Stan a watch, which he loved. It put a major dent in her savings, but she didn't care. It was worth it to see Stan as happy as he made her on a daily basis. Stan gave her a beautiful fourteen karat gold cross necklace. It had an intricate design on it with a flower in the middle, and tiny pearls throughout the gold chain. She immediately put it on, kissed Stan, and swore never to take it off.

Her Christmas celebration was somewhat different at home. When she got home on the evening of December twenty-fourth, her mother was sitting on the couch, surprisingly alone, but still with a cigarette in one hand and a glass tumbler in the other. "J'lane? Gotcha some Christmas presents," Sandy slurred as Julianne walked past the family room. As she stepped into the smoke filled room, Julianne saw a crude Christmas tree in the corner with several presents underneath it. She saw the dirt on the floor and recognized the tree as one of the shrubs that decorated the side of their house. Sandy had clearly pulled it right out of the ground and thrown a big red bow on top of it, as well as some lopsided ornaments on it. The presents underneath were wrapped in newspaper and "Happy Birthday" wrapping paper. Julianne wondered where the bow and ornaments came from since she had watched her mother throw out every holiday decoration they had after Alan left. But every time her mother tried to do something that resembled normalcy, Julianne tried to be accepting.

There were four presents under the "tree". Two had Amanda's name on them and two had Julianne's name on them. Both sets of presents were exactly the same size and shape. Julianne picked up one of her presents and looked at her mother. "Should I wait for Amanda?' she asked.

Sandy smiled. "It's not necessary," she said. "She probably won't be home until late, and I'll be sleeping, and I want to see your face when you open them." Julianne took advantage of the fact that her mother was smiling and excited, ignoring the fact that it was all most likely alcohol-induced. She began to open one of the presents, which Julianne could tell from its shape was a book. As she peeled the Happy Birthday paper back, she could see that it was the newest Agatha Christie novel. Julianne was slightly shocked – her mother had put some thought into the gift. However, as she unwrapped the next gift, she could see that her mother had Amanda in mind more than her. It was a shirt, cut so low in the front that Julianne was unsure it would cover her breasts at all. But she turned to her mother and said, "Thank you, mom. Merry Christmas," and got up to give her a hug.

Julianne retreated to her room with the book and the shirt. As she passed by the table in the hallway that used to display the dozens of

Christmas cards the Martells would get from family and friends, a tear slipped down her face when she realized only three people had bothered to send them Christmas cards this year.

Julianne flicked on her television set and lay down in her bed. Stan was going home to New Jersey that night for Christmas with his parents, and he had said that while he wanted her to meet his parents, he wanted to tell them about her first before showing up with a girl. Plus it was also the first time he had seen them in six months, and they were going to discuss with him what they had decided about their divorce, so Julianne understood and was fine with it. He would be back tomorrow, so that meant for tonight she was confined to 21 Senderfill.

After watching an episode of Scooby Doo, Julianne pulled her jar of savings out from under her bed and counted it. Four hundred and seventy-seven dollars. She had over six hundred before she bought Stan's watch, but now she just had enough for a train ticket and....that was about it. Not enough to buy a car. Not enough to rent an apartment. She sighed, defeated, and put the money back in the jar and the jar back under her bed.

Julianne laid back down on her bed, and the next thing she knew she was back in her Sarah Jean nightmare.

* * *

Her mother had just gotten done cleaning up her vomit on the bed and calming Amanda down. But while Julianne and Amanda had heard exactly what their father said and were dreading his return to the hotel room, Sandy was still convinced she had heard Alan say that Sarah Jean had been found. Julianne and Amanda didn't want to be the ones to tell their mother the grim news, so they sat on the bed, huddled together, sobbing. Sandy could not for the life of her figure out why her girls were so sad, but she chalked it up to them being in shock and continued to clean up the room and wait for Sarah Jean to return.

An hour later, Alan Martell walked back into the room. His face was shocked and pallid, paler than anything Julianne had ever seen. His eyes were completely bloodshot, and his shoulders were rounded as he shuffled past his two crying daughters on the bed and grabbed his wife in a fierce hug.

"Where's Sarah Jean?" Sandy asked, confused. "Alan, what's wrong? Where is she? Didn't you go get her?"

Alan pulled back from Sandy, his hands still on her shoulders. He licked his chapped lips and said, "Sandra, they found Sarah Jean. But she isn't...she isn't...alive." His voice faltered on the last word and he crumbled into the chair next to him. Julianne and Amanda stopped crying and watched the horrific scene unfold in front of them.

"What do you mean, she isn't alive?" Sandy said, still in disbelief.

"Sandy, I went to identify her body at the morgue this morning. And it was her. It was...it was our baby."

Amanda gripped Julianne's hand so tightly that she could barely feel it anymore. But it was nothing compared to the pain that was wrenching through her heart.

"S...someone....someone strangled her, Sandy. They r-r-raped her, and they strangled her. And they dumped her body in the woods."

Sandy Martell started shaking her head. "Stop it. Stop it, Alan! She is NOT dead! She's ALIVE! I'm fucking telling you, she's NOT DEAD!"

Alan stood up and slapped his wife across the face. Sandy was shocked; Alan had never struck her before in all the time they had been together. "She's fucking dead, Sandra. I saw her body. I saw the...bruises. On her...on her neck. And on her god damn thighs."

"Alan?" Sandy said softly.

"I just had to identify my nineteen-year-old daughter's raped and strangled body on a slab in the morgue," Alan said softly. At this, Amanda started weeping again. Sandy put her hand out to touch Alan but he pushed her away, suddenly angry. *"Do you hear me, Sandra? You didn't fucking see what I saw! I saw the bruises! I saw the damn blood! My FUCKING baby girl!"*

With that, Alan stood up and stormed out of the room, slamming the door behind him. Julianne, still clinging to Amanda, began to cry. Sandy crumpled to the floor.

They spent what seemed like an eternity in that hotel room. Julianne didn't know when day turned into night or how long it was before her father finally stormed back into the room, threw all of their clothes in bags, and announced, "Put your shoes on, ladies. We're going back to Long Island."

Amanda, Julianne, and Sandy complied. They had never seen Alan like this, and they were unsure how to handle him and did not want to set him off even more. The room was eerily silent as everyone put their coats and shoes on and traipsed out the door one by one.

Julianne heard her father speaking on the phone in hushed tones with the Vermont police before they left. She heard him tell them to call him if they discovered anything. She heard his already hoarse voice crack several times as he begged them to find his daughter's killer.

The Martell family took a turn for the worse when they arrived back on Long Island. Julianne remembered her mother being in the house for not even ten minutes when she said, "I'm going out for a drive." When she came back she had a bottle of vodka and a bag of ice. Alan, in the meantime, unpacked Sandy's bags, while Amanda disappeared into her room and locked the door behind her.

The next morning, Alan went to work. Amanda didn't come out of her bedroom, not even once. Julianne wandered around the house, lost. Sandy had vodka for breakfast, lunch, and dinner; and only knocked on Amanda's door once before retreating back to the living room. That night when Alan came home from work, he disappeared into his study for hours. Julianne listened by the door, curious.

"You have to find him. Do you understand me? I need to know," Julianne heard her father say, his voice threatening to break on every word. "I don't care how many people you've got up there looking, double it. Do you hear me? I don't care what it costs…double it."

Julianne sank to the floor. Sarah Jean was dead, and her killer was still out there. As much as Julianne tried to wrap her head around this concept, even repeating it over and over did no good at all. Although she understood the concept of death, she still had not seen Sarah Jean's dead body yet, and she half-expected her to walk through the door any minute, proving once and for all that this was just a simple nightmare.

A week later, Julianne's worst nightmares came true when Sarah Jean's funeral took place on a cold, dark afternoon. Hundreds of people came to the church – teachers, schoolmates, friends – and Julianne did not recognize a single one. Her brain was cotton, she was barely functioning. Amanda sat in the corner of the funeral home; pale, withdrawn, emotionless. Julianne longed to approach her, but Amanda made it clear that she wanted no comfort.

Julianne refused to go up to the coffin and pay her respects to her sister, because that would have made it real. Finally, Alan ushered her up to the front of the room. Her head down and eyes closed, Julianne knelt in front of the coffin and made the sign of the cross. Her eyes and heart fluttering wildly, she finally opened her eyes to see what lay in front of her.

There she was, Sarah Jean Martell, in all her morbid beauty. Dressed in her favorite pink lacy dress, her hands splayed perfectly across her chest, motionless. Julianne breathed in sharply, and forgot to breathe out. She leaned in closer to her sister, intent on taking every bit of her in. Her porcelain skin was, as usual, flawless. Her lips were ruby red and pursed as if she were just about to pose for one of her modeling pictures. Julianne reached out to touch her cheek and as soon as her hand touched Sarah Jean she drew it back, horrified at how cold her sister was.

"Daddy?" Julianne whined, finally breathing. "She's cold."

Alan began sobbing softly.

"Daddy, get her a blanket. She can't be this cold. It's not fair," Julianne continued.

A distant relative pulled Julianne away from the coffin, but her hands clung to Sarah Jean. "She's cold! She needs to be warm! Please, someone get her a blanket!"

Somewhere in the distance Julianne could hear her mother begin to sob, and that was all it took. Julianne began screaming.

"Someone, please!" Julianne cried, as she was being dragged outside the viewing room. "It isn't right! She needs to be warm in heaven! God, don't let her be so cold!" Amanda followed Julianne out the door and into the parking lot, absently petting her arm. When

Julianne was finally plunked down, she tried to go back inside, but her cousin Pat wasn't letting her.

"Julianne, calm down. Stay with me for a bit," he said soothingly.

Julianne looked at Amanda, who promptly extended her right middle finger to cousin Pat. "Let her fucking be," she said, menacingly. Pat let go of Julianne, and walked back inside, mumbling obscenities.

"Amanda..." Julianne began, breaking into sobs. She knelt down on the ground and began pounding at the pavement with her small fists until they were dripping with blood.

"Stop it, Julianne," Amanda said softly. Julianne did not stop, but instead began pounding harder. *"Stop, Julianne!"* Amanda shrieked. Julianne lifted herself off the ground and ran back into the funeral parlor.

Julianne burst into the viewing room and pushed herself through the dozens of people that were there to mourn her sister. She ran right up to Sarah Jean's coffin and threw herself onto the corpse with such force that the coffin buckled and fell to the ground. Julianne clung to Sarah Jean, shrieking and sobbing and running her hands all over her dead sister's face and body until Sarah Jean's cold, white face and pretty pink dress were streaked with Julianne's blood. Alan was beside himself as he pried Julianne off of the body and cradled her as he walked outside, burying his face in his youngest daughter's dress.

This was all Julianne remembered until the following day. She was given a sedative the morning of Sarah Jean's burial, and her only action was somberly throwing a rose onto the closed coffin as it was lowered into the ground. Amanda held her hand as Sandy and Alan threw handfuls of dirt onto the coffin, and the priest read the final rites. Again she blacked out, not remembering anything until weeks later when they woke up one morning to find Alan gone, never to be seen again.

* * *

Julianne awoke and sat up in bed with a start. She felt empty, as she so often did when she woke up from a Sarah Jean nightmare, but this time she also had clarity. What she needed to do was so clear, so plain, so simple, she couldn't believe it had taken her this long to think of it. It was the perfect plan; and even more than that, it was the perfect angle of escape.

She had to become one of Uncle Charlie's escort girls.

The New Plan

J ulianne's mind whirled with ideas. The idea of meeting new people. The idea of having power over men. But most of all, and by far the most enticing idea – making enough money to move away from her mother and sister for good. Though she also outlined the dangers of this new profession, visions of stacks and stacks of money overpowered any negative thoughts she may have had. The very idea of it all tickled Julianne with excitement, and for just a minute, a happy thrill surged through her. If she made the kind of money that Uncle Charlie's girls were making, she would have enough money to get her own apartment in New Jersey, near Stan – and by then he would be eighteen and old enough to sign the lease for her.

Stan. *Would he go for this?* Julianne wondered. On one hand, she didn't want him to know that she was sharing her body with other men; but on the other hand, she didn't want to lie to him. Stan was always stressing that a relationship was built on trust and honesty. Besides, he didn't seem to look down on what Uncle Charlie did for a living….but he didn't necessarily look up to the man either.

Julianne shook Stan out of her head. She had to think of herself first, and the disaster her life had become. Between Sandy's perverted touchy-feely male friends and the fact that she had left the oven on three times in the past month, existing in her household had become more dangerous than going to war. Was getting out of her house for good more important than the risk of losing Stan?

Julianne inhaled sharply. She couldn't bring herself to admit the answer to that question. She jumped off her bed and looked at herself in her full length mirror. Her dirty blonde hair needed to be cut, and she could stand to wear a little more makeup. She made a mental note to sneak into Amanda's room later that night and steal some mascara, lipstick, and blush. Julianne turned to the side and stuck out her small breasts. She smoothed her shirt out by the waist, put her hand on one hip, ducked her head and coyly looked upward. "I'm Julianne, your girl for the night," she said to herself seductively into the mirror.

Suddenly there was a loud crash from the front of the house and Julianne was momentarily startled. She heard moaning and figured her mother had probably missed the couch while trying to sit down again. She went to pull her mom's ass off the floor. As she passed by her mother's room, however, she heard soft snoring coming from the door, which was slightly ajar. She pushed the door open and saw Sandy passed out on the bed, still clutching an empty glass of vodka in her left hand. The moaning came again from downstairs. If her mother was in bed, then who….

"Amanda?" Julianne called down the hallway. "Is that you?" What would Amanda be doing knocking around the living room this early in the morning? Had she now resorted to coming home after the sun came up, instead of before? Julianne called out cautiously, "Mandy, what's going on?"

Julianne rounded the corner of the hallway and nearly jumped out of her skin as she saw Alan Martell collapsed on the floor of the living room, candlesticks in hand, convulsing and moaning softly. Julianne looked at her father in horror, her face twisting in pain. What was she supposed to do? What was he even doing there? The last article she read said he was in jail....was he stealing from them? Should she call 911? Could you arrest a man for breaking into his own home?

"I can't...." Julianne began to say. Alan looked so bad, Julianne barely recognized him. His once thriving hairline had receded to the middle of his head, and his formerly robust face and form had taken on a deathly gaunt look. Alan's eyes rolled into the back of his head and then slowly slid toward his youngest daughter. As they lazily came into focus, his pale lips came together in a whisper and he said, "Sarah Jean?"

Julianne's lower lip trembled and she stuttered, "D-d-daddy....wh-what are you d-d-doing here?"

Alan licked his blue crusted lips and tried to pick himself up off the floor, but his left foot failed him and he slid back down. He looked up at Julianne and put the candlesticks in a small bag that was on his arm.

"Gotta go," he said softly, pulling himself up successfully this time. Julianne stood rooted to the ground as he walked right by her, absently patting her head. With that, he was out the door.

Seven minutes later, Julianne was still standing there, completely numb. Did that really just happen? Had she imagined it? When she was able to move her feet again, she prudently looked out the window, but her father was nowhere to be seen. Julianne turned around and floated into the kitchen, her face frozen and emotionless, but her mind whirled restlessly.

How did her father get in here? Did he have a key, or did Amanda forget to lock the door when she came in at four this morning? Was he a frequent visitor to the house, or was this the first time he had been back? Wasn't he in jail? How did he get out? Did someone bail him out? Where was he getting money? Did he know that he was stealing from his own family on Christmas Day?

Instead of telling anyone, however, it just made her angrier at her family and more determined to get out. She poured herself a glass of orange juice and called Stan's parents' house to wish him a Merry Christmas.

"Merry Christmas!" A jolly female voice answered the phone. "Hi, um, can I speak to Stan, please? This is Julianne Martell."

"Hello there, Julianne!" said the happy lady, who Julianne presumed to be Mrs. Douglas. "Stan has told us all about you, and we can't wait to meet the lovely young lady who has stolen our boy's heart!"

Julianne blushed. "Thank you, Mrs. Douglas, I look forward to meeting you too. And Merry Christmas to you as well."

"Oh, you're simply too sweet. Here's Stanley. Bye, Julianne!"

Mrs. Douglas handed the phone to her son, and Julianne heard her whisper, "When can we meet her? She sounds pretty."

"Merry Christmas, Julianne, sweetheart," Stan's tenor came over the phone. "I wish you were here with me today."

Julianne's heart swelled. "Wish I were there too. It's been…less than pleasant here." Tears filled her eyes. She would not tell Stan what had happened with her father that morning. Or that her mother was still passed out and she was spending Christmas morning alone drinking orange juice in her cold kitchen because her mother had forgotten to pay the heating bill...again. "When are you coming back?"

"Tomorrow morning," Stan said. Julianne closed her eyes and breathed deeply. Another twenty-four hours here at her house. "O-OK," she choked out.

Stan immediately sensed something was wrong. "Jule, are you OK?" he asked, concerned. "Listen, if something happened, you can go stay at Aunt Debbie and Uncle Charlie's, I'll call them. I'm sure they won't mind. Seriously, it would make me feel better if I knew you were safe and happy."

Julianne sniffled. A night alone with Aunt Debbie and Uncle Charlie.....it would definitely get her one step closer to her new profession. "OK," she consented.

"Good," Stan said. "I'll call them when we get off the phone, you can go over there whenever you want."

They chatted for a few more minutes about what Stan had gotten for Christmas, and Stan said that his parents were talking again and would probably not be getting a divorce after all. Julianne was happy for Stan; at least *his* family wasn't falling apart. She hoped their kids would take their cues from Stan's family instead of hers...if what was left of her family lived to see her children.

Uncle Charlie

After Julianne got off the phone, she went for a run to clear her head. She had to put together some kind of plan for her night at Aunt Debbie and Uncle Charlie's. Of course she couldn't come right out and ask him what he did; she couldn't even let him know that she had any idea as to what he did for a living. Maybe she could ask him what his job was? Julianne wondered how he would answer her.

When she got back from her run, she scoured the outside of her house for any signs of her father, but found nothing. She showered and took out her pink and yellow duffel bag to pack for Aunt Debbie and Uncle Charlie's house.

Somewhere in the house a glass clattered to the ground, and the sound of her mother's groaning led Julianne to believe that her mother had woken up and dropped the glass that was in her hand on the floor. "Amanda!" her mother called. "Julianne!"

Julianne ignored her mother's call. She was pretty sure Amanda was going to do the same. Sandy generally called out the girls' names when she woke up groggy, flustered and confused. Sometimes, when she was especially confused, she would call out for Sarah Jean or Alan.

Amanda busted out of her room, the doorknob slamming hard against the wall. "What the fuck does she want this early?" Julianne heard her hiss as she stomped into the bathroom. "Merry Christmas, Amanda," Julianne called out as Amanda passed her room. She winced, waiting for the backlash. The stomping stopped momentarily, and there was a slight pause as Amanda said remorsefully, "Merry Christmas, Julianne."

The corners of Julianne's mouth turned up just slightly. At least Amanda hadn't cursed her out.

Several minutes later the entire house was buzzing with sluggish activity. Amanda was in the shower, and Sandy was in the kitchen making coffee and her morning vodka on the rocks. Julianne was just about finished packing. She looked under her bed at the canister of money and decided to take it with her. She shoved it all the way to the bottom of her bag.

Skipping down the hallway, Julianne called out, "Bye, Mom! I'm going to Stan's for the night!"

"OK dear," Sandy called back. "Tell Stan and his family that I said Merry Christmas."

Julianne shook her head. She loved how her mother tried to act all maternal and proper when it came to her boyfriend and his family. As if she really gave a shit about any one of them.

As she opened her front door to begin the long walk to Stan's house, she was met with a blast of cold air. Somehow the temperature had dropped significantly since she had been out running several hours earlier. It even felt like it might snow. It was going to be a long walk, but the end result would be well worth it. She'd learn more about Uncle Charlie's business....and most importantly, she'd be out of her house. Her nose began to run as she walked, and she wiped at it with her gloved hands. The gold cross that Stan had given her the other day felt bitingly cold against her skin underneath her shirt, but she pressed on. She tried to think warm thoughts; tried to think about Stan holding her in his arms. She thought about the first time they had sex, which was just a few days earlier. Julianne thought it would be a lot more exciting, and she was somewhat disappointed. But Stan seemed happy, and all she wanted to do was please him, so if that was what it took, she was more than willing to do it. Her limbs flooded with warmth as she thought about the undeniable look of love in Stan's eyes after they were done. Julianne heard it got better the more you did it, so she hoped that was true. After nearly an hour of walking as fast as she could through the bitter wonderland, she finally saw Aunt Debbie and Uncle Charlie's house in the distance. Relief washed over her.

Julianne shivered as she held her hand up to ring the doorbell, but before she could press it, Aunt Debbie flung the door open and said, "Good Lord, child, you're going to catch your death out there! My God, I'm surprised you don't have frostbite!"

She hurried Julianne through the door, into the warm house, taking her duffel bag and setting it down in the foyer.

"What can I get you? Hot chocolate? Tea? Coffee?" Aunt Debbie was ready to wait on Julianne hand and foot, as usual. "Come on, lovely, you've got to drink something to warm your bones up!"

"I'll have a hot chocolate," Julianne mumbled, her jaw half-frozen shut. Aunt Debbie ushered her into the kitchen where she got to work making Julianne's hot chocolate.

"Stan will be back tomorrow, so you can sleep in his bed tonight, is that alright?" Aunt Debbie chattered. Julianne nodded, still numb. Aunt Debbie continued, "I told Stanley that you can stay here any time you want, even after he leaves, and I'm going to tell you the same thing, dear. Whenever you want, you hear me? Uncle Charlie and I are always happy to have you."

Had Julianne been thawed out, her eyes might have filled with tears. It was nice to be wanted. Instead of admitting how desperately happy she was to feel welcome, she just mumbled, "Thank you, Aunt Debbie."

Julianne wondered just what Stan had told Aunt Debbie and Uncle Charlie about her and her home life and family. Julianne guessed he had to have filled them in a little bit, because they were always more than amenable to Julianne staying over, even on school nights. They never made her feel as if she were a guest, but rather part of the family. Julianne was grateful for their hospitality and even more grateful that they never asked her a single question.

"Do you want to watch some TV with me and Uncle Charlie?" Aunt Debbie asked, setting a steaming cup in front of Julianne. Julianne smiled, the warmth inside her not just coming from the heat in the house, but from the love she felt for Stan's aunt and uncle.

"You can bring the hot chocolate in the den, sweetie," Aunt Debbie said, pouring herself some sparkling water. Julianne looked at Aunt Debbie's jewelry, which seemed to have gotten more sparkly since she knew what kind of money paid for it. A ruby and amethyst necklace on an eighteen karat gold chain, that hung perfectly between Aunt Debbie's fake perky breasts; large gold hoop earrings with tiny diamonds set into the circle every couple of centimeters; a silver and gold bracelet made up of interlocking hearts that dangled delicately from Aunt Debbie's slim wrist; a silver pinky ring that was worn on Aunt Debbie's right hand, with a small pale pink stone in it; and the most impressive piece of all, her wedding ring. The ring had to be at least three karats, maybe four. It was so big that when the light hit it in a certain way the flash was almost blinding. The band was gold, and squiggly like a snake, with a very intricate design that went around the outside of it. When Julianne had complimented it on one of her first visits to the house, Aunt Debbie had held her hand out in front of her, cocked her head to the left, and said, "It's the best present I've ever gotten, and worth every penny. You should see the looks I get from other girls when I'm out." Her eyes sparkled almost as bright as the diamond.

Stan had told Julianne in private a few days earlier that when they got married her ring would be bigger than Aunt Debbie's. That was the first night that she and Stan had made love, and Julianne remembered wishing that it were five years into their future and that she were already Mrs. Stan Douglas.

Julianne settled into the comfortable armchair in the den as Aunt Debbie flicked on the television. "Where's Uncle Charlie?" Julianne asked.

"He had to run out," Aunt Debbie said. "He should be back within the hour."

Julianne dozed off almost immediately. She felt Aunt Debbie put the heavy multi-colored quilt which was usually draped over the couch on top of her, and tuck in the sides. Aunt Debbie was so nice. Julianne figured it was probably because she had no kids of her own, so doting on her and Stan was almost like a treat for her.

She was awakened by the sound of Uncle Charlie slamming the front door and announcing cheerfully, "I'm home!" Julianne stirred, turned her head in the direction of Uncle Charlie's voice, and smiled.

"Well, well look what we have here, a Christmas surprise!" Uncle Charlie chuckled, walking in Julianne's direction. Uncle Charlie looked the same as he always did...not too old, not too young, but somewhere in the middle, although Julianne could never guess quite where the middle was. Late thirties? Mid-forties? Aunt Debbie was significantly younger than him, at least by six or seven years, this much Julianne knew. Uncle Charlie had on his signature track suit, and as Julianne looked him up and down she wondered just how many of those ensembles he owned. She never saw him in anything but track suits. Like Aunt Debbie, Uncle Charlie's collection of jewelry was quite impressive, especially for a middle-class man. Around his neck he wore a thick gold chain with an enormous gold cross at the neck. He had the same kind of golden rope entwined around his left wrist. Similar to his wife, his wedding band was eye-catching to say the least. A thick gold band wound its way around his left ring finger, and it had a large diamond inlaid in the center.

While Julianne was admiring Uncle Charlie's display of gold, Aunt Debbie suddenly appeared. "Julianne is going to stay here with us tonight," she explained to Uncle Charlie, with what Julianne thought was a knowing glance.

"Of course, she's always welcome here," said Uncle Charlie. He started to take his coat off and Aunt Debbie grabbed it from him to hang it up.

"What happened?" she asked in hushed tones as he walked into the kitchen. "Where did you go? It's Christmas Day..."

"I know that, Deb. My kind of work doesn't exactly take a holiday. There's a lot of lonely men on Christmas, you know? I tried to be as quick as I could. Just had to pick up one of the girls who doesn't have a car and bring her over to Johnny Doyle's house," Uncle Charlie explained.

Their voices lowered to a mumble until Julianne couldn't hear anymore. She turned her attention to the television and focused her eyes on it while her mind whirled with questions. Do the girls get more money on holidays? How many guys ordered girls on Christmas Day? Did the girl Uncle Charlie had to drive not have a car, or not have her license? She hoped it was the latter, which would mean that she had a fighting chance of being one of Uncle Charlie's girls. Of course the biggest question that danced through her mind was, how was she going to let Uncle Charlie know that she not only knew what he did, but she wanted to be a part of it?

"Julianne, dinner!" Aunt Debbie called from the kitchen. Julianne threw off the quilt and yawned as she walked toward the scent of delicious smelling food. She loved that Aunt Debbie cooked almost every meal, and remembered a time when her mother used to love cooking for their family. She often thought Stan took it for granted.

"Mmmm, smells delicious, Aunt Debbie! What are we having?" Julianne asked as she padded into the kitchen. "Spaghetti and meatballs with garlic bread," Aunt Debbie answered. Julianne sat down at one of the three place settings at the table and put her napkin on her lap. Before picking up her utensils she closed her eyes and inhaled deeply. She almost didn't want to breathe out, she was so content. Julianne wanted to savor this perfect moment forever – a home cooked meal, a warm house, dinner with a mother and father figure who actually cared for her – it was a scenario she had just about given up on. She carefully exhaled and opened her eyes. "Thank you for having me," she said politely to Uncle Charlie and Aunt Debbie.

Uncle Charlie paused and pointed his fork at Julianne with a smile. "What did I tell you, missy? You're always welcome here."

The meal was quiet but comfortable. Julianne told Uncle Charlie and Aunt Debbie what her mom had gotten her and Amanda for Christmas. Aunt Debbie asked where her mom and sister were going tonight, and Julianne said, "Probably nowhere. They'll probably just have dinner at home." It was a lie, and even though Aunt Debbie probably knew that, she hoped she sounded semi-convincing. She knew that it would be just another night in the Martell household: Amanda would walk out the door to make another night of bad decisions, and her mother would drink herself into oblivion until she passed out on the couch. She sighed heavily, thinking once again how sick of her family she was. The sight of her father trying to lick his dry, cracked lips in their living room that morning flashed through her mind, but she pushed it out and focused on the task at hand – figuring out a way to get Uncle Charlie to hire her.

There were no opportunities during the meal, but after dinner when the three of them retreated to the living room for television, Julianne caught her big break. While walking behind Uncle Charlie, he reached into his pocket to pull his handkerchief out, and a small business card fluttered to the floor. Julianne picked it up and turned it over in her fingers. In small, precise cursive, it said "Charlie's Angels" and underneath it was a phone number. Just below that was a grey halo and a set of angel's wings.

Julianne trembled with excitement when she realized what she had picked up. This was it, her chance! "Uncle Charlie, you dropped your...."

Uncle Charlie turned around and saw Julianne with the small white business card in her hands, and his eyes nearly popped out of his head. "Thank you, Miss Julianne," he said, swiping it out of her hands. He looked at her for a minute, as she looked up at him with her blinking blue eyes. The corners of her mouth turned up ever so slightly, and in that moment, he knew that she knew exactly what was going on.

"Darling, what should we watch tonight? Do you want to watch a sitcom or *It's a Wonderful Life*?" Aunt Debbie chirped, settling into her chair.

Uncle Charlie, not taking his eyes off Julianne, said, "Let's watch, *It's a Wonderful Life*. It's only on once a year, and it's one of my favorites."

As Aunt Debbie flicked through the television channels, Julianne and Uncle Charlie were locked in a gaze behind the couch. Julianne did not want to look away for fear that she would appear weak and scared, and that was the last thing she wanted. She wanted Uncle Charlie to know that she was for real, that she wanted to work for him. Now she just had to find a way to open her mouth and say so.

Uncle Charlie studied her, this skinny girl that he had come to care for like a niece, and wondered just what his nephew had actually told her. But he knew that she knew. He knew by the look in her eyes and by the way she was not taking her gaze off of him, that Julianne indeed knew what he did for a living. He studied her harder, trying to figure out if she was irritated—or—was that interest he saw in her earnest stare?

As if reading his mind, Julianne pointed at herself and with all the courage she could muster, mouthed, "I want to."

Uncle Charlie's eyes almost popped out of his head for the second time in five minutes. Julianne wanted to be a prostitute? Was this for real?

"Charlie, come sit! Julianne, where are you? The movie's starting!" Aunt Debbie said, not turning around.

Uncle Charlie looked at his wife, then back at Julianne. She was still staring at him, waiting for an answer. He looked her up and down, sizing her up. She wasn't nearly as pretty as some of his top girls, but she was young. And there were many men who wanted young girls. Her breasts were smaller than most of the girls he employed, but he could have someone teach her how to play them up. After several quick thought processes, he suddenly went from Uncle Charlie to Businessman Charlie. He narrowed his eyes and mouthed back at Julianne, "Talk later."

Julianne finally lowered her eyes and took a deep breath in. She was trembling inside worse than she ever had before, but it was over. She had asked him. And he had said he would talk to her about it. She went around the side of the couch, smiled at Aunt Debbie, and snuggled under the warm quilt once again.

Julianne was far too nervous to even pay attention to the movie. She was so excited she could barely stop fidgeting. After about an hour she heard Aunt Debbie's light feminine snore coming from her left side, and she turned her head to see Aunt Debbie fast asleep. Uncle Charlie, on the contrary, was wide awake, his eyes black and beady as he focused on the television.

When the credits rolled, Uncle Charlie nudged Aunt Debbie. "Sweetie pie, go lay down. I'll be inside in a few minutes, let me just get Julianne into bed and shut the Christmas lights off around the house."

Aunt Debbie got up from the couch wordlessly, kissed Julianne on the top of the head, and headed off toward the bedrooms. No sooner had the door shut behind her then Uncle Charlie turned to Julianne and demanded, "How did you find out? Did Stan tell you?"

Stay cool, Julianne.

"He did. But please don't be mad at him. We were trading family secrets, I told him mine and I guess he felt he had to tell me his," Julianne explained quietly. "I swear, Uncle Charlie, I'm not going to tell a soul."

Uncle Charlie narrowed his eyes. "Family secrets? What kind of family secrets could you possibly have?" he asked suspiciously.

Julianne stared at him coolly. "My sister was murdered and they still haven't found her killer, my other sister is a drug addict who fucks everything in sight, my mother drinks three meals a day, and my father left us...for a heroin addiction."

Uncle Charlie was impressed with her determination and nerve. None of his girls had ever spoken to him with such impudence, especially not the young ones.

"What do you want to know?" he asked.

"Everything," Julianne said slowly. "How many girls are there, how many nights a week do they work, how old are they, how old are the men they are with? And most importantly, how much money do they make?"

"I have anywhere between twenty and thirty girls at a time," Uncle Charlie began. "Sometimes girls try it out and decide it isn't for them, sometimes their boyfriends catch wind of it and don't let them come back anymore, so I've got kind of a revolving door. But never more than thirty. They work as many nights a week as they want. Some girls have full time jobs and do this on the side. Some girls do this five or six nights a week as their only source of income. My younger girls, like you, are still in school so I have to be extra careful with them. Technically you're supposed to be eighteen to do this...well, not that there's an age limit that makes this legal, but if you're under eighteen you can get in much more trouble. And so can I, if we get caught."

Julianne listened intently. "What do the men make you do?"

Uncle Charlie grimaced. "Don't you think this is crossing the line? I feel kind of weird talking to you about this, seeing as you're my nephew's girlfriend –"

Julianne interrupted him and she hoped she sounded as confident as she intended to. "Uncle Charlie, with all due respect, we crossed the line about ten minutes ago. Please don't think of me as Stan's girlfriend. Can we think of this as an interview?"

Once again he was impressed, so he continued. "Mostly the men just want sex. No more, no less. Straight up, simple intercourse. Sometimes they want a blow job to go along with it. I always ask my clients exactly what they are looking for, so I know which girl to pair them up with. For example, I have a guy who likes to get really nasty with girls, and not every girl likes that. I usually give him my girl Dottie, because she can handle him, and she likes it rough as well. Some guys want you to dress up, that costs extra. Some guys want you to dance. Some guys want you to talk dirty to them. But it's all negotiated beforehand, that's what I do. I talk to my girls and I find out what they will and won't do, and I pair them up with the right men. There's no shame in doing less. It's a personal preference. And like I said, most men just want sex."

"How much money do they make?" Julianne asked, fascinated.

"It varies, really. To be honest, the more you do, the more money you get. I am very fair to both my clients and my employees. I—"

"How much, Uncle Charlie?" Julianne interrupted again. This was what she was waiting for.

Uncle Charlie looked her straight in the eyes for at least a minute before he opened his mouth and said, "A girl like you could probably get anywhere from sixty to seventy-five dollars a night, to start. If you're good and you stick with it you could eventually make up to four hundred a night, easy.."

Julianne's mouth fell open. She knew she looked foolish but she didn't care. This was it, her ticket out of Carrollton. She would move away from Long Island, away from her family, away from.....

Stan. She loved him, that was for sure, but she couldn't stay here. If he wanted to come with her, then so be it; but otherwise, she had to go. She probably wouldn't even have to work for Uncle Charlie that long, maybe a year, tops. She'd make a ton of money and then split. Uncle Charlie said that girls were coming in and out all the time, so what did it matter?

"Listen, Julianne. I don't want you to discuss this with Stan. Yes, he knows what I do, but I think he'd be quite irritated if he knew I was propositioning you."

"Propositioning…me?" Julianne could hardly believe her ears.

"Yes, Julianne. Propositioning you," Uncle Charlie said, then broke into a smile. "Would you like to come and work for me?"

Julianne could barely contain her excitement. She jumped up and hugged Uncle Charlie around his neck and shrieked, "Yes! Oh, thank you, Uncle Charlie! You won't regret this, I promise!"

Uncle Charlie disentangled her and put his hand over her mouth. "Hush, Julianne! We *cannot* let Aunt Debbie know about this arrangement either! Even more so than Stan, do you understand?"

Julianne sat back down on the couch. "Yes," she said somberly, but she couldn't stop the sides of her mouth from twitching. "Doesn't she know…"

Uncle Charlie cut her off, nodding. "She knows. She knows more than most. But she'd be furious with me if she knew I was employing you. She doesn't like to know my girls. She likes to stay very far removed from the whole thing."

Julianne emphatically bobbed her head up and down and said, "I got it, Uncle Charlie. I swear I won't tell a soul. You can trust me."

"I know," Charlie said, "That's why I asked you." After a slight pause he added cautiously, "I know you ain't got the best deal at your house, but there's no chance of your mother finding this out either, is there?"

Julianne harrumphed sarcastically. "I didn't come home for a week when I first started dating Stan and she didn't even ask where I was. You think she's going to care if I'm gone for a few hours a night? The only time she'll notice is when someone's not there to refill her drink."

"OK. I am going to have one of my girls who's been with me a long time call you and give you a more proper training session. Her name is Dawn. Here," Uncle Charlie said, shoving a business card and a pen at her, "Write your number down on this. I'll give it to her."

Julianne scribbled her home phone number and handed the card back to Uncle Charlie. "When?"

"Two days," he said. "You're going to go out to lunch with her and ask her any questions you can think of about the job. It might be easier for you to talk to her because she's a girl, you know? Whatever you want to know, you ask her, and she will be able to answer your questions. Dawn's been with me for thirteen years, she knows all the tricks of the trade. I'll make sure she lets you know how to handle a man if he gets unruly, and how to make sure you give him exactly what he pays for and nothing more. 'Cause sometimes they try to get more, and they'll take advantage of the young girls."

Julianne nodded, trying to take it all in. She was also still trying to figure out how she was going to hide this from Stan.

"One more question, Uncle Charlie," she asked. "Where do we go, you know, with the men?"

Uncle Charlie had all the answers. "They are required to provide a space. Usually they will rent a hotel room, sometimes if they don't have a wife they'll bring you back to their place. All places have been checked out and okayed by me ahead of time, but you are to call me on your way to wherever you are going and let me know exactly where it is, so I can let *you* know that it's been checked out beforehand. But in the beginning, for the first couple of months or so, I'll follow you in my car. Probably longer with you, because you're so young, and because you're kind of family. So I'll be outside the entire time you're in the hotel room with the client."

Julianne nodded. She felt safer and safer as Uncle Charlie explained it all. This was a totally legitimate business, she thought. Besides, Uncle Charlie cared about her. He wouldn't put her in any danger. He knew Stan cared about her and would be devastated if anything happened to her.

Stan's face kept popping up in Julianne's mind as she digested all of this information. She knew he would be livid about her sharing her body with strange men. But she was so utterly desperate to get out, her morals were slowly shrinking further and further into the distance as the dollar signs flashed in her eyes.

"Alright, now you try and get some sleep, Miss Julianne. Tomorrow we don't discuss this. Not to Stan, not to Aunt Debbie, not to anyone. The next time you will mention this is when Dawn calls you in two days."

Julianne nodded, afraid to speak for fear that she would sing with happiness. She could hardly contain the excitement bubbling from her every pore. She had a job that was actually going to make her enough money to get out of Carrollton.

Dawn

T he next morning Julianne woke up to something fluttering over her face. She opened her eyes quickly and saw Stan standing over her, kissing her on her cheekbones lovingly. Seeing him filled her with warmth, and she immediately threw her arms around his neck and hugged him with all her might. "I love you, Stan," she said into his neck. "I love you too, Julianne," he said back. She felt a pang of guilt but quickly pushed it away.

They sat together on the couch for hours and cuddled, while watching TV. Uncle Charlie was up to his usual antics, fielding phone calls and shouting out girl's names, while Aunt Debbie was cooking in the kitchen. Julianne got a secret thrill every time she heard him mention a girl's name and how much money the girl was going to make. She couldn't wait to count her bills next weekend and see how much would be there.

Stan was confused as to why Julianne didn't want to stay for dinner, but she insisted that he drive her home. She said that she wasn't feeling well, but really she wanted to make sure that she was at her house from morning until night tomorrow to wait for that call from Dawn. "But Aunt Debbie will make you some broth," Stan protested.

"I just want my own bed, sweetie. I'm sorry. I'll come back tomorrow night if I'm feeling better," Julianne said.

To his dismay, Stan drove her home. When she walked in the door, the house was eerily quiet, but upon further investigation she found her mother in the master bedroom, drinking a glass of vodka and staring at the television. It wasn't turned on. "Mom, do you want me to turn on the TV for you?" Julianne asked. Sandy turned her head and stared at Julianne blankly. "Sarah Jean, the TV's off," she said softly. Julianne swallowed the lump in her throat, crossed the room, and turned on the television. The soft noise filled the room and gave it a slight vibe of life. Semi-satisfied, Julianne turned to walk out the door, but not before she heard Sandy mutter, "Thanks, Sarah Jean."

Once in her room with the door safely locked, Julianne took out her jar of money. She placed it on the nightstand next to her bed and looked at it, imagining the overflow that was about to happen. Before she knew it she was asleep.

The next morning dawned cold but sunny. Julianne was awakened by the sun gently lapping at her face through the dirty blinds that hung in her room. Her eyes shot open as she remembered what day it was – the first day of her new job training with Dawn and the rest of her life.

She rose from bed and turned on the water in the shower. Julianne wanted to make sure she looked her absolute best so she could impress Dawn later. She carefully washed her hair, shaved her legs, and scrubbed every inch of her body. She ran her hand up the side of her wet naked thigh and slowly moved it toward the middle of her body, imagining that it was one of her clients. That was what Uncle Charlie called them, right, clients? Stan's face popped up in her mind but she determinedly shoved the image out. Julianne plunged her fingers into the small dark space between her legs and twisted them around. She tried to pretend it felt good, but she actually didn't feel anything. She figured it would be different when it was someone doing it to her. She silently thanked God that she had chosen to lose her virginity to Stan, so having sex with strangers wouldn't hurt as much.

Julianne turned off the shower, stepped out, and stood in front of the mirror. As she wiped the mist off the glass, she jumped back slightly because she thought she saw Sarah Jean's face, but it was just her own. She stared at herself in the mirror for several long minutes and then said out loud, "I want to do this."

Now is not the time to have an attack of conscience, Julianne told herself. *Uncle Charlie has been doing this for years. It's perfectly safe. He is not a criminal and neither are you. You are providing a service. If you think about this as a job and a business and not anything else, you will be just fine.*

Julianne used the blow dryer to dry her hair and styled it with Amanda's round brush. Then she slowly crept into Amanda's room and borrowed her sister's overflowing makeup case, carrying it out the door and down the hall without a sound. She had never worn makeup other than a bit of mascara before, but she figured now was as good a time as any to play the part she was going to play.

First she put on a little bit of pancake, rubbing it under her eyes and nose the way she had seen Sarah Jean and her mother do. Then she used Amanda's blue eye shadow to carefully fill in her eyelids. The black eyeliner was a little tricky, she had a difficult time drawing a straight line on her upper lid, but with a few Q-tips and fill-ins of the eye shadow she looked like a seasoned professional. Before putting on some rouge and mascara she carefully curled her eyelashes so that they looked perfectly round and lifted. The final touch was her mouth. Julianne lined the outside of her lips with Amanda's dark brown lip liner and then colored it in with a dark pink shade. She puckered her lips and kissed the air in the mirror, then smiled at her reflection. Not a supermodel, but a vast improvement. Julianne decided that she would definitely be investing in makeup after her first appointment.

She stealthily put the makeup case back in Amanda's room and snuck back into her own room. Now for her outfit; this was going to be the difficult part, because most of her wardrobe consisted of jeans, sweaters, and long sleeved shirts. She had never been one to flaunt her figure, though she did have the beginnings of one under most of what she wore.

Julianne stared at the twelve pairs of jeans that were on hangers in front of her. What if....yes, she had an idea. She quickly pulled one of the pairs of jeans off the hanger and ran into the kitchen with them. Fumbling through the kitchen junk drawer, she found what she was looking for and held them up with glee. Holding the scissors with care, she scurried back to her bedroom to begin her fashion project. A quick glance at the clock told her it was only ten in the morning, so she still had plenty of time. She cut and snipped with care, and after about twenty minutes put the scissors down and held up her creation. Jeans....with holes cut in them. Perfect! Julianne slipped them on and looked in the mirror. They were casual with just a little bit of an edge. Besides, she had sworn she saw this look on the cover of a magazine the other month.

Now it was time for a top. Without hesitation, she pulled out from hiding, the top that Sandy had given her for Christmas. It was a blue, white, and pink paisley print, and when she put it over her head and turned around she was instantly happy with what she saw. She put on a pair of old blue platforms which she knew were out of style but they looked all right; plus, they were all she really had. She made another mental note to go shopping with one of her first paychecks as well, also mentally noting that she would be making more than enough money so she could spend some of it on the side.

Julianne stood back and looked in the full length mirror and breathed in. She looked phenomenal. Her small but perky breasts were accented perfectly in the revealing top. Her honey blonde hair hung straight down past her shoulders and had just a slight flip on the bottom. The jeans snugly fit her tiny curves in all the right places, and she had cut the denim in just enough spots so that there was minimal flesh showing, but still enough for people to take notice. She smiled coyly and her blue-grey eyes sparkled with mischief. "Hi, Mr. Smith," she said softly, trying out her sexy voice. She imagined herself pushing Mr. Smith on the bed and crawling on top of him and seductively unzipping his pants. She imagined his hands slowly finding their way under her top and inside her bra. She imagined him...

The shrill ring of the phone cut Julianne's daydream short. She bolted for the kitchen and picked up the phone and breathlessly said, "Hello?"

"How are you feeling, any better?"

It was Stan. She loved that he had called to see how she was feeling. She loved that he recognized her voice when she answered the phone. For what seemed like the millionth time in the past twenty-four hours she shoved her love for Stan out of her mind and said, "Yes, baby, I'm feeling better, thank you."

"Do you want to see a movie today?" he asked.

"Sure, later," Julianne answered.

"What are you doing now?" Stan questioned.

"Nothing, just…hanging out with my mom, having tea," she lied.

Stan was silent, and just when Julianne feared he was going to catch her false story, Sandy poked her head into the kitchen and slurred, "Sunshine, who's on the phone?"

"It's Stan, mom," Julianne said, thanking her lucky stars that her mom had appeared almost on cue.

"Tell that lovely boyfriend of yours that I'd love to see him soon," Sandy said.

Stan must have heard her because he bought the lie and said, "OK, enjoy your morning and call me later. Want to go around six?"

"Sure," Julianne said, and forced a smile. "I'll call you later."

They said their goodbyes and hung up.

"So what's new?" Sandy asked Julianne, filling the tea kettle with water and taking a bottle of vodka out of the freezer.

"Not much, mom. Stan and I are going to the movies later," Julianne said. "Is that OK?" Julianne didn't know why she bothered asking her mother's permission, because half the time Sandy didn't know where Julianne was, but it made her feel like an ordinary teenager for about five seconds, but only for five seconds.

"Of course," Sandy said absentmindedly. "Can you just tell Sarah Jean that I'm not feeling very well and I'll have to take her into the city tomorrow?"

Julianne shook her head and her eyes filled with tears. Her mother was beginning to really lose it. "Mom, Sarah Jean is dead," Julianne said through clenched teeth.

Sandy whirled around and stared at Julianne with unblinking eyes. Her mouth fell open in a tiny O and she started gasping for air. She clutched the countertop and slammed her eyes shut, her knuckles getting whiter by the second. Suddenly she started laughing hysterically and fell to the floor. Julianne watched her, horrified.

The tears began to slip faster and faster down Julianne's cheeks as she wondered how long her mother had left before she needed to be committed, and what would happen to her and Amanda when that time came. She prayed that it wasn't before she made enough money to move herself far, far away.

The phone rang again and Julianne gulped and answered it. "Martell residence," she said softly. Sandy was still laughing and gasping for air on the floor, and Julianne twisted her body around into the other room hoping that the telephone cord would follow her.

"Hi, can I speak to Julianne please?" came a tiny female voice on the other line.

Julianne's heart began to pound. "Speaking."

"This is Dawn," the perky voice said. "I work for Charlie. He gave me your number."

"Hi, Dawn," Julianne said.

"So, we need to meet today. What time are you free?"

"Whenever," Julianne breathed. "The sooner the better."

"Great!" Dawn exclaimed. She sounded really sweet, Julianne thought. She imagined Dawn as a tall blonde with blue eyes. "Where do you live?"

"Senderfill and Bounty. In Carrollton."

"OK, do you want to meet up at Lou's Diner?" Dawn asked.

"That's fine," Julianne said. She mentally calculated it would take her about forty-five minutes to walk there. Almost as though she had read her mind, Dawn asked, "Do you have a car?"

Julianne exhaled. "No," she said.

"No problem. I'll just pick you up, is that okay?"

Julianne smiled. This wasn't so bad. "That would be great, Dawn. I'm at 21 Senderfill."

"Cool, I'll swing by in about an hour. See you then."

Julianne hung up the phone and looked at her mother again, who was in the fetal position on the kitchen floor, still laughing like a certified lunatic. She was now clutching at the side of her silk robe so forcefully that it was beginning to fray. Another tear found its way down Julianne's cheek, but she wiped it away and sniffled. She couldn't afford to ruin her makeup now, after it had taken her so long to put it on. Though she felt bad about leaving her mother laying on the floor, she had slowly been having feelings of disconnect from her mother and Amanda for the past several weeks and it didn't bother her nearly as much as it used to.

Julianne waited on the couch and watched television until Dawn arrived. When she heard the sound of a horn in the driveway, she picked her purse up off the armchair and ran out the front door before her mother could ask her where she was going.

The silver Z-28 Camaro that sat in her driveway was more than impressive. Julianne's eyes rounded at the sight of it, and she remembered when her family could afford to drive impressive cars. She ran toward it and opened the passenger door with a flourish and got into the warm automobile.

She turned to her left to look at her mentor and was shocked beyond belief. Dawn was not even close to what she had expected. Instead of the statuesque blonde that had been dancing around in Julianne's mind, there was a short, striking, long-haired brunette. Dawn had a perfect pointy nose and her pin straight hair hung almost into her lap. Her flawless red fingernails sat daintily on the stick shift, and her matching red lips were pursed in a precarious smile. She wore a full-length mink coat that gave her some bulk, but Julianne could tell underneath it she was just as tiny as her voice was on the phone. Her makeup was unblemished; it was so natural it barely looked like she was wearing anything at all. The only thing about Dawn that Julianne had pictured correctly was her eyes. They were a perfect piercing blue that Julianne could only compare to the ocean. Dawn was most definitely a natural beauty, and it was no wonder that she was Uncle Charlie's top girl. Julianne almost felt that given the chance, she too would probably sleep with Dawn.

"You gonna stare or you gonna say hello?" Dawn said playfully in a perfect Long Island accent.

"Hi," Julianne breathed. She had never seen someone so beautiful.

Dawn started backing out of the driveway and drove off in the direction of Lou's Diner. "God, you're young," she said, eyeing Julianne.

Julianne looked down at her legs. All of a sudden her outfit, which had been fabulous a few hours ago, seemed childish and amateur next to Dawn's spectacular ensemble.

"No, honey, it's not a bad thing, believe me. The guys are gonna love you," Dawn said, giggling. It was infectious. Julianne started laughing, even though she didn't know exactly what she was laughing at.

Before long they parked at the diner, and they both got out and walked inside. Once they were seated and Dawn took off her massive fur coat, she leaned across the table and grabbed Julianne's hands in her own.

"Listen to me, honey. I'm gonna tell you straight up, this business is just like any other. There are upsides and there are downsides. I've been doing this for thirteen years, and let me tell you, it was rough in the beginning. I lost a lot of family members and friends because they didn't believe in the lifestyle. But I'll tell you what I got instead – money. Piles and piles and piles of money. And I wouldn't trade it for anything."

Julianne took a deep breath. "I have no family," she said. "And all I want is money. I want to move away from here."

Dawn looked at her sympathetically. "Oh honey, you're so little, and I am sorry that your life isn't what you thought it would be. But let me tell you what. From now on, think of me as your big sister, OK?"

Julianne looked into her sparkling blue eyes with such longing that she thought Dawn would see right through to her desperation. "I've always wanted a big sister," she whispered.

The waitress came to their table, and Dawn ordered them both a coffee. Once the waitress had gone, Dawn said, "OK. So, why don't we start out with me running you through a typical appointment?"

Julianne nodded and took a sip of her coffee.

"First what happens is a man, let's call him Mr. Jones, will call Charlie and say to him that he wants to make an appointment, and he'll give him the date and time. Sometimes he'll give a few days notice; sometimes he'll give only an hour or so. You'll give Charlie your schedule ahead of time, let him know how many nights a week you wanna work, and he will know which girls are available for the time that's been requested. So let's say Mr. Jones will ask for a young blonde, and you're available. Charlie will call you and say something like, Mr. Jones, eight o'clock, Morley Motel. That means that you are to meet Mr. Jones at the Morley Motel at eight o'clock, obviously. I always show up a little earlier, because sometimes the men are early, but you are not under any circumstances to be with them any earlier than the time that Charlie says because they pay by the hour, do you understand?"

Julianne nodded, enthralled. Dawn flicked her long brown hair behind one shoulder and continued.

"So you go into the room with Mr. Jones at eight. It's up to you to bring a watch, because most appointments only last for one hour. If they pay for more than one, Charlie will say it on the phone, he'll say eight to ten instead of just eight. If he just says the start time it means they only paid for one hour.

"Now, when you get inside the room, you are not to speak. Mr. Jones will tell you what he wants you to do. Most of Charlie's clients have been working with him for years and they are respectable, and Charlie won't put you with a new client for a while most likely. Most of these men just want blow jobs and sex. Occasionally they'll want you to dance for them. Can you dance?"

Julianne cleared her throat. "I...I guess I could work on it."

"I would recommend working on it. You got a mirror in your bedroom at home?" Dawn asked.

"Yes."

"Practice. To be honest they just want you to move your hips a little bit and gyrate, but they won't last more than a few minutes without putting their hands on you. So you dance a little, then he pulls you onto the bed. He will tell you if he wants a blow job, and if he does, you suck his dick. If he tells you he just wants sex, then you take your clothes off and have sex with him. Have you ever had sex before?"

Julianne nodded, unable to find her voice.

"Good, at least it won't be your first time. Men can always tell when it's your first time. So then you have sex with him, as many times as he wants. Some men only want to have sex once and you may be done in thirty minutes. That's a lucky appointment, cause you'll still get paid for the hour. But some guys will push it until the last minute. That's when it's up to you to say politely that it's time for you to leave. Am I going too fast? Do you have any questions?"

Julianne cleared her throat again and took another sip of coffee. "I, um…I don't have a car. How will I get to wherever I am supposed to meet the guy?"

"I didn't have a car when I first started either," Dawn admitted. Then with a wink she added, "But I bought one six months later. In that case, you will probably just wait at the end of your street and Mr. Jones will pick you up there."

"What if…what if… do they hit?" Julianne asked her greatest fear.

Dawn sighed. "I've encountered a few that did. But like I said, when you're just starting out, Charlie will put you with guys he knows and trusts, guys that have been clients for a while. He will also probably sit outside whatever hotel you're at just to make sure that you come out exactly after an hour. If you don't, he'll come in. By the time you go out with a new client you'll know how to handle yourself, I promise. Charlie followed me around for a year and a half before he trusted me enough to go out on my own."

"Do they...bring protection?"

"It's a requirement. If they don't have it, you are allowed to walk out. Despite this business not being exactly legal, Charlie runs it as clean as it can get, I promise. That's why all the girls want to work with him. How did you meet him, anyway?" Dawn asked.

Julianne looked to the side, her eyes filling with tears. "I...I date— well, Stan is my boyfriend."

Dawn's blue eyes widened. "Oh, damn," she breathed. "That could get messy."

There was a slight uncomfortable silence, and then Dawn continued. "So listen, honey. In the beginning, after you're done having sex with Mr. Jones, when you walk outside, you'll probably see Charlie waiting somewhere. Once you see him, you can get back in the car with Mr. Jones and he will take you home. OK?"

The lump in Julianne's throat was so big she could barely breathe, so she fluttered her eyes and bobbed her head twice.

"You do drugs?" Dawn asked, staring hard at her.

"No," Julianne whispered.

"Good. You're better off. The girls who do drugs in this business are the girls that don't last. Now, do you have any questions?"

Julianne's mind was racing. She had a million questions, everything from how did she hide this from her mother and boyfriend to when did she get paid.

Dawn looked at her, concerned. "You look a little pale, honey. Listen to me, this might all seem a little scary, but isn't any new job? Please look me in the eyes for a minute."

Julianne raised her head and looked at Dawn's beautiful face. "I promise you," Dawn said, "You are in no danger at all, do you hear me? I have been with Charlie since I was your age, and look at me now. I have a beautiful car, a beautiful apartment, beautiful jewelry; I have everything I've ever wanted."

"Do you have a boyfriend?" Julianne croaked.

Dawn rubbed her hand and looked down. "Occupational hazard," she said. "I'm gonna be honest with you honey, it's near impossible to date someone. I tried it when I was in my twenties, but the guy always ended up finding out what I did, and he didn't want to share me. And can you blame him? This profession is not for the weak. It's also not for the girl who wants to settle down with a family. Now, I've known many girls who worked with Charlie for three, four, even six years, and then met a guy and wanted out. And Charlie lets them out, with no problem. Most people are in it for a quick buck, they really are. And it's one of the only ways to make one. Honey, if you want to do this for two years and then get out, no one will look at you different. No one will even know."

"How old are you?" Julianne realized her questions were not even making sense. They were not even about the job. She just wanted to know more about Dawn.

Dawn smiled. "If you promise not to tell anyone, I'm thirty-four. But if anyone asks, I'm twenty-eight. Only Charlie knows the truth."

"Have you ever had sex with Charlie?" Julianne asked, somewhat emboldened.

Dawn had been taking a sip of her coffee and she nearly choked on it and quickly put it back down on the saucer. "Never," she said. "Charlie is a complete gentleman, and he is one of my nearest and dearest friends. He loves Debbie, and even though his job is not as respectable as a banker's, he has been faithful to her for all these years, of that, I am certain."

Julianne was silent. She thought about what Stan was doing at that moment. She wondered if he was calling her house. She wondered if her mother was even answering the phone.

"I wanna go back to the drugs topic for a minute, honey," Dawn said, her voice low. "There are some rules."

"Do I have to do them?" Julianne asked quickly.

"Not ever," Dawn said firmly. "Many of these men will be hopped up on God knows what. They'll do cocaine, they'll do meth. They'll offer it to you. Julianne, I beg of you… *do not touch it*. It's the only way you will be able to keep your mind about you and know what you're doing. You need to keep your eye on the time and your eye on the ball. And the ball is the amount of money you'll be making. You start doing drugs, you're fucked. Charlie has fired girls because he found out they were doing drugs with clients. No drugs…got me?"

"Got it," Julianne echoed. "What about alcohol?"

"Sometimes they bring some. If you want to drink it, you drink it. If you don't, you don't. If you do drink it, don't get out of control. I always limit myself to two drinks. Any more than that and I can get a little unruly," Dawn explained. "But seeing as you're really too young to drink at all you should probably just stay away completely. I mean, these guys will know you're underage and they might try to ply you with alcohol to take advantage. If I were you, I wouldn't take a drink at all." Julianne figured that Dawn knew what she was talking about, so she added "don't drink alcohol" to her growing mental list. Julianne began to wonder about the pay.

"You get paid after the job," Dawn said, as if reading Julianne's mind. "Mr. Jones will give you x amount of dollars, and you keep your cut and you give Charlie his cut when you see him. Charlie said he is going to offer you for eighty-five dollars an appointment to start, and you'll get twenty-five of it."

Julianne's mouth dropped open. "Twenty-five dollars just for one hour?"

Dawn smiled. "Told you it was worth it."

"I used to barely save up twenty-five dollars for one week of work," Julianne laughed.

"Better get a new piggy bank," Dawn said. "Cause yours is about to bust open, my dear."

Julianne smiled. She was beginning to feel a little more at ease. "How much do you get per appointment?"

Dawn breathed out heavily. "I don't want you to compare yourself to me, honey. I've been doing this many, many years. I'm an expert."

"How much?" Julianne asked again.

"Three fifty an hour."

Julianne was aghast. "Three hundred and fifty? And how much of it do you get?"

"Two hundred."

Julianne didn't know what to say. She didn't even think her father made that much per day when he was working, let alone per hour. "And how many appointments do you do per day? Or...per night?"

"Well," Dawn explained. "When I started out I was only working nights. But then, Charlie started getting guys that wanted lunch visits, you know? So I do a lot of day appointments too. I'd say that I do anywhere from three to four appointments a day. When you get to be good, and if clients like you, they'll actually request you. I have many regulars."

Julianne quickly did the math in her head. If Dawn did three appointments a day at two hundred an appointment....she was making well over three thousand dollars a week. Stan had been way off in his calculations. Of course, she could never hope to make as much as Dawn, but still...

"Thank you for meeting with me," Julianne said.

Dawn looked at her and cocked her head. "You remind me a lot of myself when I was your age. What's your story? What's a nice girl like you living in a nice house like that wanna get into this for?"

Julianne had forgotten that she actually did live in a nicer part of town, and when the house had been under monthly upkeep it actually was rather notable. She wanted to tell Dawn her story, but was wary. She had just met her.

"Listen, honey," Dawn said, grabbing Julianne's hands over the table again, "You don't have to tell me anything you don't want to. But tell me something. Just a little something. Like I said, we're gonna be sisters. I have to know something about you."

Julianne smiled weakly and looked around. She didn't recognize anyone in the diner. There were only a dozen or so other people sitting at tables, and they were paying no attention to her and Dawn. She started to feel a little more comfortable. She really liked Dawn. Dawn seemed to have her best interest at heart, and she had been doing this for thirteen years. Julianne felt that she could be trusted.

"I–I have two sisters. Well, I had two sisters. My sister Sarah Jean was killed about a year and a half ago. Now I have one sister, her name is Amanda, and she....she's not really on the right path. Well, I guess neither am I," Julianne laughed dryly. "My dad is—gone. And my mom is crazy." She paused and looked up, tears threatening to spill over. "And I need to get out. I need to get away from here before something else happens. I've already lost half of my family, I can't be around to see the other half fall apart."

Dawn nodded knowingly. "Honey, listen to me. I never even knew my father. My mother met him at a sit-in, they were both high on LSD, and they fucked in a bathroom. My mother always told me that I was the worst thing to happen to her. She's still rotting away in the same house I grew up in, bathing in alcohol and marijuana. I haven't spoken to her in twenty years, and I'm just fine. Sometimes, the people we think we need the most, we don't need at all. Especially when they are bad for us."

Julianne was feeling closer and closer to Dawn by the second. "My mom drinks all day every day. My sister Amanda has sex with all these boys and does more drugs than I care to know. I'm so terrified that one day, one or both of them is just going to die and I'm going to have to clean up the mess–just like I had to clean up the mess when my father left and Sarah Jean died."

"Wait a minute," Dawn said, strumming her red fingernails on the tabletop, "Your sister is the one that went missing at college last year?"

Julianne slammed her eyes shut, and saw Sarah Jean's face in front of her. Smiling, hair flowing, eyes twinkling. "That's us."

"My God, honey. I'm so sorry. I followed that story and I hoped that that guy was found. I am so sorry for you and your family, I really am." Dawn said.

Julianne went rigid. She could not be like this every time Sarah Jean's name was mentioned. It was one thing to bathe in her own memories of Sarah Jean but she hated when other people talked about the tragedy like they were connected to it or had even an inkling of what her family had gone through. Imminent tears welled up in her eyes, but she squeezed them back and vowed that from there on out, her family would not make her emotional. "It was a long time ago," she said to Dawn with renewed strength. "I try not to think about it."

Dawn nodded. "You're a very strong girl, Julianne. Which makes me feel like you're going to be perfect for this job."

Julianne smiled. "I want to make you proud, and Uncle Charlie. I want to make as much money as you, and be Uncle Charlie's next top girl. After you, of course."

Dawn smiled. "I like your determination. You'll have to work hard, but...you're pretty enough. I think you can do it.

"Now listen," Dawn continued. "Charlie told me that you were getting a code name. Which didn't make sense before, but now that I know you're dating his nephew, it makes complete sense. He doesn't want Stan to hear him booking you. He is going to call you Daisy. Is that OK?"

"Daisy," Julianne said out loud. "Daisy, Daisy, Daisy." She smiled. She liked flowers, and the name was feminine, sexy, and completely neutral. It was perfect.

"OK, good, so that's settled. Now listen, can Charlie call your house? Or will your mom pick up and ask questions?"

"No way," Julianne said, rolling her eyes. "If anything, she'll mistake him for one of her millions of boyfriends."

They both giggled. "We have more in common than you think, Julianne Martell," Dawn said. "Now the next thing we need you to do is get rid of that boyfriend. Seriously."

Julianne smiled uneasily. She loved Stan. She didn't want to have to get rid of him.

Julianne's First Time

L ater that day, when Julianne and Stan were out watching a movie, Dawn's comment came back to gnaw at her. It gnawed at her as they walked to the movies, it gnawed at her while they watched, and it gnawed at her while he held her hand. She became so uncomfortable with him that halfway through the movie she shook his hand off. Concerned, Stan turned to her and said, "What's wrong?"

"Nothing," she whispered, shrugging. "My hand is just getting clammy." Stan turned his head back toward the movie screen. That night Julianne asked Stan to drop her off at home. Stan said nothing, but thirty seconds later sighed exasperatedly. "Julianne, what's going on? You haven't stayed at my house since I've been back from home, you won't hold my hand in the movie theater....what's up?"

Julianne knew that if she were ever going to perfect her acting skills, now was the time. With all the innocence she could muster, she turned to Stan and looked at him imploringly with her big grey-blue eyes. "What are you talking about? I'm sorry I haven't stayed over, it's not you I swear, it's just–my mom is–not really doing so well," Julianne said, looking down. It wasn't exactly a lie. Julianne was fairly certain her mother was months away from losing her alcohol-saturated mind. "She's just been...out of sorts. And Amanda isn't home to watch after her, you know, so I have to. It might be like this for a while. I'm sorry."

Stan's expression instantly softened, and he took Julianne in his arms. "I'm sorry Jules," he said. "I'm sorry life is so tough right now. I wish I could make everything better. Do you want me to stay over at your house? Do you think that would help? Do you think your mom would allow it?"

Julianne digested this, and considered it briefly. But she dismissed the idea and Stan by saying, "I don't think it would make my mom happy. She's always been a private person, and I just don't think she'd want a non-family member seeing her this way." The truth was, Julianne didn't want Stan seeing her mother this way. She also couldn't bear to have Stan see what actually went on in her house on a daily basis. Telling him about it and exposing him to it for an hour at a time over tea was one thing, but having him witness an overnight firsthand was something else altogether.

They made out for a while, and Julianne got out of the car in her driveway. She watched with a sinking feeling as Stan's car rolled away. Her heart and stomach ached with hurt and guilt. She felt awful lying to Stan, but there was no other way. Besides, soon he would be going away to college and it would be much easier for Julianne to lie about her whereabouts.

Julianne walked inside, her stomach churning. Her brain hurt from conjuring lies. To her surprise, Amanda was sitting on the couch next to her mother, who was passed out. Amanda turned to look at Julianne as she walked by the living room and Julianne could see the sadness in her sister's eyes. She knew she shouldn't, but she asked anyway. "What's wrong, Amanda?"

"Something's not right with mom," Amanda said, sounding very small. Julianne looked at her mother, who was sitting upright next to Amanda, eyes glassed over, looking straight ahead. Sandy was the epitome of "The lights are on, but no one is home."

"Maybe she should quit drinking for a day and her brain will dry out," Julianne said bitterly.

Amanda sighed deeply and hung her head back down in her lap. "Not going out tonight?" Julianne continued.

Amanda shook her head no, and put her hands over her mother's hands. Sandy remained comatose. Julianne couldn't watch anymore. "Maybe you should make her drink some water," was all she said as she made her way down the hallway and into the sanctity of her bedroom.

Locking the door, Julianne began her task for the night – spicing her bland wardrobe up and making some suitable outfits for her new job. Julianne kept her money jar on the corner of the nightstand as inspiration. She snipped and sewed a few pairs of jeans and cut up some shirts in all the right places. Before long she had about six different ensembles that she was pleased with.

The phone rang early the next morning. Julianne jumped out of bed to get it, excited that her day was beginning already. She was only mildly disappointed when she heard Stan's tenor on the other end. He asked how her mom was doing, and she brushed him off within minutes. As soon as she hung up the phone, she immediately called Dawn.

"Hello?" came the pert Long Island accent from the other end of the phone. Julianne instantly relaxed upon hearing Dawn's voice.

"Oh, hi, honey," Dawn said. "Charlie said you'd probably be starting tonight, do you think you're ready?"

Julianne breathed in excitedly. "Yes!" she exclaimed. "I picked out a bunch of outfits last night that I'm going to wear."

"That's excellent, honey. I think Charlie will probably put you with Richard tonight. He's a Thursday regular, real sweet and gentle. I promise. And he likes the young ones, so Charlie will probably pitch you," Dawn explained. Julianne took note of the new language that she would need to learn.

"Is he....old?" she asked.

Dawn giggled. "No, sweetie. He's about forty. Which I guess, when you're my age, isn't old...but to you, he might be. Doesn't look old though. And he's no drama. He has no wife, no kids. Just a nice hard-working guy who likes to pay for sex. Do you have condoms?"

"No," Julianne's face burned. "I thought..."

"They are supposed to bring the protection. But I should have told you yesterday to always come prepared, because sometimes the client will conveniently "forget" and then expect you to have unprotected sex with him. Of course you wouldn't, but then he'll get mad, and demand his money back. It's just easier to come prepared. Do you want me to pick you up so we can run to the drug store and get you a few things? Condoms, chewing gum, lipstick or something?"

Julianne loved Dawn. She absolutely loved her. "That would be great," Julianne said enthusiastically. "But what if..."

"If he's gonna book you for tonight, he'll call between noon and one. I'll see you in an hour, honey."

Once again, Dawn was a vision of perfection. She was wearing a short fur coat this time, with a tight pink shirt that accentuated her perfect breasts and supertight dark denim jeans. She wore dark pink platforms that Julianne thought were out of style, but somehow Dawn pulled them off as vintage. Her hair was pulled up into a ponytail that hung straight down her back. Her eyes looked even bluer than they had the day before, accented with thick black eyeliner and pretty pink eye shadow. Julianne wondered if Dawn woke up in the morning looking as flawless as she did all day.

Dawn paid for all of Julianne's drug store necessities. She got her a jumbo pack of condoms, a nice shade of lipstick, an eye shadow, some pink bubble gum, and a little pouch to carry it all in. Julianne thanked Dawn, who waved her off as she handed a small card to a man that was staring at her the entire time they were in the store.

"What was that?" Julianne asked incredulously. "What did you just give him?"

"My card, honey. This isn't something you can advertise on television. Gotta do your own promotions in this business. If you last longer than six months, Charlie will give you your own card," Dawn said.

"How do you know he wasn't a cop?" Julianne felt foolish for asking so many questions, but they all seemed important and she figured she should know the answers since it was her new profession.

"Because I know all the cops in this town," Dawn laughed, winking.

Julianne was floored. Uncle Charlie was cleaning up. No wonder he had such a successful business and never got caught – the Carrollton police were his clients! Julianne was dying to ask Dawn how many people she had slept with in her life, but thought it might be going just one step too far. Besides, she figured she'd get an approximation sometime soon.

Some hours later, Julianne found herself standing in the dark at the end of Senderfill Road, waiting for Richard. Charlie had called her at exactly noon, and when she answered the phone he said, "Hi Daisy. Richard is picking you up at six-thirty sharp, Langley Motel, Drop off around eight o'clock, Twenty-five to you, sixty to me." And then he promptly hung up without waiting for a response. Julianne phoned Dawn right after and she decoded the whole thing. As Dawn had predicted, Richard was her date that evening. He would be picking her up at the end of her road at half past six. He would bring her to the Langley Motel, where they would have sex from approximately six forty-five to seven forty-five. He would then drop her back off at the end of her street at eight and give her eighty-five dollars. When Julianne would meet up with Uncle Charlie the next morning, she would give him sixty dollars and keep twenty-five. It seemed simple enough.

A sleek black sedan pulled up next to her at exactly half past six. The window rolled down and a good looking dark haired man looked her up and down and said, "You Daisy?"

Julianne nodded, afraid to speak.

"Get in," he directed. Julianne walked to the other side of the car and let herself in the passenger side. As he drove away, Julianne suddenly realized with a small amount of fear that she had gotten into a car with a complete stranger – something her parents had always warned her not to do. As well as something that had led to the demise of her eldest sister.

"So, you're the new girl, huh?" Richard asked, his eyes fixated on her legs. Julianne was glad she had worn the short skirt, even though the lower half of her body was frozen solid because of the subzero temperature outside.

She nodded again.

"Do you talk? You don't have to be afraid, Daisy. I'm not going to hurt you. Me and Charlie go way back. I'm one of his best customers. You can trust me," Richard said soothingly.

Julianne's naivete got the best of her and she uncrossed her arms and put them down at her side. "This is, my first—" She began.

"I know, beautiful. Don't worry, I'll be gentle," he said, running his fingers down the side of her face and barely brushing against the top of her breast, which was peeking out of a shirt she had stolen from Amanda's closet.

When they got to the Langley Motel, he instructed her to stay in the car while he went to get the room. Several minutes later, he was back, waving a key at her through the windshield. "Come on, pretty. We're all set!" he said.

He opened the door for Julianne and she got out of the car. Her legs felt as if they were made of lead as she followed Richard to the room where they would do the deed. Suddenly her mind began racing and her heart thudded in her chest. Was this right? She forced her eyes shut and tried to see whose face came to her first.

Shockingly, it was Dawn's. With her sea-blue eyes she winked at Julianne and said, "Make me proud, honey."

Julianne took a deep breath and stepped into the dimly lit hotel room. Richard was suddenly behind her, massaging her shoulders and breathing into her neck. "God you're so young. And so damn hot," he whispered. "I'm going to make you scream like no man has ever made you scream before. Do you want to fuck me?"

Julianne closed her eyes and started shaking and just when she thought she was about to lose it, she got a grip and turned around. "Yes, Richard. I want to fuck you," she whispered, putting her face into his cheek.

Richard groaned and picked Julianne up, kissing her and undressing her as he made his way to the bed. Julianne actually didn't find it hard to get turned on, as Richard was a good-looking guy and clearly knew what he was doing with a woman. Once she was completely naked, he stood back and looked at her while he put the condom on. "You're perfect," he said. "We're definitely going to do this again next week."

And with that he was on top of her, pushing himself inside. It hurt Julianne a lot; Stan was not this rough, but she tried to turn her cries of pain into sounds of ecstasy. Julianne slammed her eyes shut and tried not to think about what was happening. She tried to think about piles of money. She tried to think about the beautiful apartment she was going to buy herself. She pictured the brand new car that she was going to get, even nicer than Dawn's. She saw herself on shopping spree after shopping spree, buying the most expensive clothes in every store. She wanted fur coats and expensive shoes, just like Dawn.

And then just like that, it was over.

With a final grunt, Richard picked himself up off the bed and went into the bathroom. Julianne stayed on the bed, very still, unsure of what she was supposed to do. It had definitely not been an hour. Was the whole appointment over? She lay there for a good five minutes, until Richard came out of the bathroom, grinning. He was still completely naked.

"You can get dressed, cupcake," he said. "Or at least cover yourself up. Give me twenty minutes and I'll be good to go again. And then I'll drive you home."

Julianne slowly put the covers over herself. Without dressing or covering himself up, Richard turned on the television and sat in the chair next to the bed. He and Julianne watched an old sitcom without speaking to one another for a while and then, like clockwork, twenty minutes later he turned to her again with lust in his eyes. Julianne decided it was better the second time.

As she was getting dressed, Richard threw four twenty dollar bills and one ten dollar bill on the table. "For you, pretty," he said.

"I don't have any change," Julianne said, staring at the cash.

"You don't need any. Give Charlie his sixty, and you take thirty. Little extra, this being your first time and all, and I do want you to keep coming back," Richard said, his grin infectious. Julianne smiled back at him and said, "Thank you, Richard."

"No, cupcake, thank *you*."

Richard continued being a gentleman as he helped Julianne out of the hotel room and back into the car. Julianne saw Uncle Charlie's blue Chevrolet across the parking lot, and so she was more comfortable getting back into Richard's car. She became one hundred percent comfortable when the blue Chevy started up and followed them out of the parking lot all the way to Senderfill Road, where Richard stopped. The blue Chevy drove right by.

Richard kissed her gently on the cheek and said, "See you next week, Daisy." Julianne feebly thanked him again, got out of the car, and limped toward number 21.

Deceit

T he next morning, Julianne felt less bad about what she had done the night before. She almost didn't even remember it, save for the stinging pain she felt between her legs. She stared at the ninety dollars on her dresser and once again envisioned a pile of cash. She walked into the kitchen, took an aspirin out of the medicine cabinet, and phoned Stan.

"Good morning!" Stan answered the phone, thrilled to hear Julianne's voice as usual.

"Hi, Stan," Julianne said, with a lump in her throat. "How was your night?"

"It was OK, uneventful," he replied. "I think Uncle Charlie has a new girl, he was out most of the night, that's usually what he does when he follows someone new."

"Oh, really?" Julianne answered nonchalantly. Before Stan could say anything else she quickly changed the subject. "What are you up to today?"

"Nothing," Stan answered, "Want to go to lunch?"

"Sure," Julianne replied. "Can we do it around one?"

"No problem," Stan said. "I'll pick you up around then."

Julianne hung up, consumed with guilt once again. She hoped she was working tonight but also wondered what she would tell Stan. He was going to start wondering where she was every night. She decided to talk to Uncle Charlie about it when he called her for that night's assignment.

Julianne phoned Dawn when she was done showering, because Dawn had told her to call the next morning and let her know how the evening went. Dawn was pleased to hear that not only had the evening gone well, but that Julianne had gotten a tip on her first night. "He's great, I told you," Dawn said knowingly. "And the tip means he likes you, so that means he'll ask for you every week. I told you, he likes your type. He was a regular of mine, until I got too old for him." Dawn laughed her perfect tinkling laugh, and Julianne emulated her.

"I just–I just don't know what to tell Stan," Julianne said quietly.

Dawn sighed. "This is why having a boyfriend is no good," she said. "I'd talk to Charlie about it. See what he recommends. Maybe he can even keep the kid busy, it is his nephew after all."

"I was going to talk to him next time he called. Do you think he'll call me today?" Julianne asked.

"If he doesn't call you by one, then there's no job," Dawn said, "It's a waiting game, honey."

"Did you go to school when you did this at first?" Julianne asked.

"Yeah," Dawn said, "Wasn't easy. Especially when some of my clients were my friend's fathers. But you have to keep in mind all the time, *always* be discreet. I graduated high school, but never went to college. Why would I? I made all the money I needed. All the money I ever will need."

Julianne nodded, and when she realized Dawn was waiting for an answer she said, "OK."

"You'll be fine, honey," Dawn said. "Trust me. I really feel that we have a connection, me and you. And if I could do it, you can too."

Talking to Dawn made Julianne more sure every minute that she was doing the right thing. Dawn was everything Julianne hoped to become through her new profession: beautiful, rich, and lusted after by men of all ages.

The phone rang shortly after noon and Julianne rushed to answer it. Unfortunately her mother got to it first. "Hello, Martell residence," she slurred. "Stan? Is that you? Yes, Julianne is right here. Tell your parents I said hello!"

Julianne shook her head and rolled her eyes. She couldn't count how many times she had told her mother that Stan's parents were in New Jersey and he was living out here with his aunt and uncle, but her mother's brain retained very little these days. Julianne started to think that it was lucky if her mother even remembered her name in the morning. Sandy handed the phone to Julianne with one hand and took a sip of her drink with the other.

"Hello?" Julianne said timidly as she took the phone.

"Is that your mother?" Uncle Charlie's voice asked on the other end.

"Yes." Julianne said quietly.

"Shit, I'm sorry. Stan told me she was bad but....Shit."

Julianne remained mute.

"Anyway," Uncle Charlie continued, clearly uncomfortable with the silence, "Got another one for you tonight. Another good guy, I promise. Johnny, picking up at quarter past seven, Langley Motel, drop off eight forty-five."

Before he had a chance to hang up, Julianne spoke up, "Uncle Charlie?"

"Yeah, hon?"

Julianne frowned. "I..I'm getting a little nervous about what will happen if Stan finds out I'm doing this. He is going to start wondering where I am every night."

"Listen, hon. It's up to you how many nights a week you think you can get away with lying to him. I'll try and find something to keep him busy tonight, but obviously I can't do that every night. But if you want to only work two or three nights a week, that's fine, just let me know. And I know you still got school and all. I'm sure you know the more nights you work, the more money you make. So you let me know, OK?"

"Thank you, Uncle Charlie," Julianne said.

"No problem," he said, and with that he hung up.

Julianne had lunch with Stan and realized she would only be able to lie to him about her whereabouts for two to three nights a week maximum. She also figured that she only had another few months before Stan went away to college, and then she could work as many nights as she wanted. She had counted on making her piles of money immediately, but at the same time she didn't want to lose Stan, so she compromised. She knew she would have to quit her job at the ice cream parlor, but decided she would tell Stan that she had to work there a few nights a week and hoped that he wouldn't ask to pick her up from work.

"I'm going to have to work at the ice cream place a few nights a week," Julianne heard herself lying to Stan.

"Why? What happened to Maryann?" he asked, inquiring about the night-shift girl.

"She can't work all the time anymore, I guess," Julianne said.

"OK. You want me to come pick you up when you're done?"

"Nah, it's no problem," Julianne waved him off. "I like the walk home anyway. Gives me time to think."

Stan looked at her inquisitively. "Are you sure?"

"Absolutely," Julianne said, shaking her head for emphasis. "It will be getting warm soon anyway."

"It's only January," Stan said with a chuckle.

"Well still. It'll give me time to work out my legs before summer."

"Your legs are perfect," Stan said, leaning over the table and kissing her on the nose. His lips felt foreign and stiff after Richard's had been all over her last night.

Changes

Hours later she was dressed in tight jeans and yet another low cut shirt, courtesy of Amanda's closet, waiting at the end of Senderfill Road. Uncle Charlie's blue Chevy drove by and he waved at Julianne. She nodded at him in return, too cold to remove her hands from her pockets.

Shortly after, a silver SUV pulled up and a man much older than Richard rolled down the window. "Daisy?" he asked.

Julianne nodded and got in the car. Once inside she turned to look at her suitor for the night, taking in his grey hair and old man smell. She figured he had to be in his sixties, and wondered how men that old could still even have sex, but figured as long as he was paying money there was no reason for her to ask questions. "Hi, there, sweetheart," he said, taking in every inch of her body.

Julianne zoned out as they drove to the Langley Motel. She answered his questions with short answers and nothing more. Johnny repeated the same scenario that Richard had the night before, getting out of the car to rent the room and then calling her out of the car. She walked into the hotel room, noting the blue Chevy parked several spaces away. Feeling more comfortable with every step she took, she shut the door behind her and began the night's work.

Johnny's lips burned into Julianne's skin as he kissed her face and neck, and Julianne felt as if he was scarring her and everyone would be able to see her sins. But when it was over, just like Richard the night before, Johnny gave her a five dollar tip. Julianne looked at her thirty dollars and realized she had made sixty dollars in two hours work, and suddenly her burning skin didn't matter anymore. When Julianne got home she put the sixty dollars with the other sixty from Richard to give to Uncle Charlie the next time she saw him.

The following day when Uncle Charlie called, Julianne said, "I'd like to do three nights a week, Charlie."

"Sounds good, Julianne," Uncle Charlie said. "Are you coming over tonight then?"

"Probably," she said. "I'll bring your money when I come."

"Go to the bathroom when you get here and leave it under the hand towel," Uncle Charlie instructed.

When Julianne got to Stan's house that night, she immediately excused herself and went to the bathroom. As soon as she came out, Uncle Charlie went in. The rest of the night was just as most other nights at Stan's, they all ate dinner together, and then she went to sleep for the night with Stan. Even though they made love that night, Julianne was unreceptive to Stan's romantic gestures. She went through the motions with an immense amount of guilt.

For the next few months, Julianne adopted a schedule. She would work two weeknights and one weekend evening, and Stan believed that she was working at the ice cream parlor. Uncle Charlie was careful not to book her too late on school nights, and once a week when she went to Stan's house she would leave her weekly earnings for Uncle Charlie in the bathroom under the handtowel. Julianne and Dawn talked almost every day, and they had become very close. They laughed and giggled about their nightly appointments and went shopping together every week. Stan knew nothing about her new friendship, whenever Julianne went out with Dawn she made up an excuse about having to clean her room or tend to her mother.

Julianne was incredibly pleased with the amount of money she was saving. When she had been working at Seth's she was saving just about twenty-five dollars a week; with her new job she was saving about five hundred dollars a month. She calculated that if she could work five nights a week after Stan left for college, she would only have to work through her senior year of high school and then she could move as soon as she graduated. Sometimes she wondered what Stan would say when he found out she had all this money, but she figured she would save that for when the time came.

Life at the Martell house was becoming increasingly difficult, however. Sandy glided around the house with blank, unstaring eyes, always clad in a bathrobe. She only showered when Julianne helped her do so, and only spoke when it was to ask someone to get her a drink. Julianne refilled her mother's glass but did so with a heavy heart. She knew she was killing her mother, but in a way she didn't care anymore. As far as she was concerned, Sandy died the day Sarah Jean went missing. Amanda rarely came home at all. Julianne didn't ask but figured she had a boyfriend. She also figured Amanda's boyfriend was beating her up when she saw bruises on the inside of Amanda's arms, but when she told Stan about the bruises he shook his head, looked down, and said, "Heroin."

Julianne shook her head adamantly. "Amanda would never do heroin," she said, her voice shaking. She closed her eyes and shook her head, a move that she did so often when there was a strange man entering her, and simply blocked it out. Her dreams of Sarah Jean were now few and far between; instead she dreamed of her new life far away from Long Island, complete with all the money she could ever want. As much as she wanted to leave, she wondered how she would walk away from such a lucrative job, but figured she would save those decisions for later.

By the time the snow started to melt and the birds began chirping again, Julianne had saved almost three thousand dollars. She counted her money nightly, almost scared that it was going to disappear if she didn't check it daily.

One afternoon as she was sitting in her bedroom watching television, Amanda burst into her room unannounced. She saw forty dollars sitting on Julianne's dresser and eyed it hungrily. "Where did you get so much money?" she asked, narrowing her eyes. Julianne swallowed the lump in her throat.

Amanda leaned down and snatched the shirt that Julianne had borrowed the night before off the floor. "I was looking for this. Why is it in here?"

Julianne could not speak. Amanda's eyes opened slightly and her lips curved into a sinister smirk. "Taking a page from the older sister's book, are you? Good for you. Hope Stan is enjoying my wardrobe. Ask next time, OK bitch? And if you're stealing the money, let me know where you're stealing it from. I could use a few bucks myself."

With that, Amanda snatched up a twenty from Julianne's dresser and walked out the door with her shirt. Julianne let her have it. She knew Amanda had no job and she had no idea what she did for money. Plus, Julianne had more than enough and could afford to give her sister half a night's earnings.

Things got even better, mid-summer, when Uncle Charlie gave Julianne her own business card and raised her rate. She was now making a hundred and ten dollars per appointment, with Uncle Charlie getting seventy-five and her getting thirty-five. Julianne passed her card out whenever she went out with Dawn, to everyone from the grocery checkout guy to the men on benches outside the mall. Julianne had developed a regular clientele, and Richard and Johnny had become two of her best and most preferred customers. Occasionally she would come across the type of men that Dawn had warned her about – some tried to push the time limit, and some offered her drugs. She knew that Charlie was always waiting outside, because she saw him, so she had no problem getting stern with someone who was trying to take advantage of her. Julianne always refused the drugs that were offered to her. She let the men do them, and laughed inside when it affected their performance. The clients still had to pay though, sex or not.

Stan had found out that spring, he had been accepted to Montclair State University in New Jersey, which was exactly where he wanted to go. Throughout the summer he was careful not to be too exuberant about his acceptance, because he was sad to leave Julianne, but Julianne was happy for him. She wanted him to follow his dreams, especially because when he left, it would leave her free to follow hers. Her long term plan was to continue working as one of Uncle Charlie's girls until Stan was done with college, and then marry him, move to New Jersey, and be a stay-at-home mom. She never let Stan know how much money she had been making, and carefully hid her stash away on the rare occasions whenever he came over to her house. Julianne had ultimately decided that eventually there would be the right time to tell Stan that she had been working for Uncle Charlie, but it was most definitely not now. And there probably wouldn't be a right time until after they were married.

The summer was difficult for Stan and Julianne's relationship. They had been fighting quite a bit, mainly because he would accuse her of not being into the relationship anymore. She would tell him he was crazy and that she loved him, and eventually his fears subsided. Julianne knew she had been a shitty, absent girlfriend, but she silently prayed that Stan loved her enough to stand by her until they could really be together. She kept telling herself that even though she was earning more money than she could have ever dreamed of, that the job was temporary. It had to be.

* * *

The day that Stan left for college was extremely difficult for both of them. Julianne had slept at Uncle Charlie and Aunt Debbie's and when she woke up, Aunt Debbie had chocolate chip pancakes waiting for the two of them in the kitchen. Julianne had cried herself to sleep the night before because she knew she was going to miss Stan, and woke up with puffy eyes and a mild headache.

"Julianne, I'm serious," Aunt Debbie said as she poured her a glass of milk, "I better see you here at least twice a week, do you understand? You're the daughter we never had."

Julianne's eyes filled with tears and she nodded. She knew that what she would miss most about Stan was the sense of stability he brought into her otherwise chaotic life. Between her murdered sister, her absent father, her alcoholic mother, and her prostitution job, there was nothing about Julianne Martell's life that had any sense of conventionality except for her boyfriend and his family. Who would she turn to when Amanda's pregnancy test finally came out positive? Where would she run when her mother was flinging glass tumblers across the kitchen because she had just discovered there was no more vodka in the house? Of course Julianne knew she could always go over to Aunt Debbie and Uncle Charlie's, she almost knew she had to in order to keep up appearances, but being around Uncle Charlie had started to make her feel tainted. She knew he knew she was anything but pure, and shame had started to consume her every time she saw him. Uncle Charlie and Dawn had told her time and time again, "Julianne, it's a job. It's a simple business transaction, and you have to look at it as such. If you don't, if you let your brain get the best of you, you'll never be able to do it." Julianne had learned to simply put herself on autopilot the moment she got into a client's car, and her mind went somewhere else completely while her client was having sex with her. But for some reason she still felt like she needed a good scrubbing more often than not.

Julianne often found herself wondering what her life would have been like if Sarah Jean never died. She imagined it would be nothing like it was now.

When Stan's parents' car rolled into the driveway, Julianne began blubbering like a baby.

Stan put his face close to Julianne's and whispered, "Listen to me. I'm going to call you every day, do you hear me? It will be almost the same as it is now. We'll get to talk every single day, we just won't see each other every day, OK?" He wiped the tears from under her eyes and kissed her nose, but it only made her cry harder. Stan caressed the side of her face and pulled her close to him.

Julianne nodded, tears sliding down her cheeks and snot dripping from her nose. Aunt Debbie handed her a tissue as Stan's parents honked the horn impatiently.

"Shit, they're not even going to get out of the car?" Aunt Debbie commented loudly. Stan disentangled himself from Julianne and started helping Uncle Charlie bring his boxes and suitcases down to the car.

"Don't they want to meet me?" Julianne asked, confused.

"Don't pay them any mind," Aunt Debbie said, with the slightest hint of bitterness in her voice. "My sister became a completely different person the day she married that horrible man. I prayed every night that they would get divorced, but it appears she's changed her mind."

"But she was so nice to me on the phone that time when I called..." Julianne said, still puzzled.

"She was probably trying to piss him off," Aunt Debbie spat.

Aunt Debbie held Julianne's hand as they watched their men pack up the station wagon. Julianne strained to see Mr. and Mrs. Douglas' faces through the windshield of the car, but there was too much of a glare. How could they hate her without even knowing her?

"Do they not like me?" Julianne whispered. Maybe Stan had told them about her family history...

"Don't be silly," Aunt Debbie scolded, squeezing Julianne's hand tighter. "I'm telling you, Betty is a whole different person when she's around that man. I'm glad they're not getting out of that car. The very sight of Jack makes me sick."

Uncle Charlie and Stan put the last of Stan's boxes in the car and were shutting the back hatch. They came back over to the porch and Stan pulled Julianne close to him and squeezed her so tightly she thought she was going to burst.

"I love you, Julianne, and I'll see you in two weeks, OK?" Stan whispered into her ear. Stan had already planned his first trip back to Carrollton, providing school did not get in the way, and said he would continue to do so every two weeks until Julianne got a car.

"I'll be counting down the minutes," Julianne whispered back, her tears salty on her lips. Mr. Douglas leaned on the horn again, its impatient tone blaring up and down the street. She pulled away from him and stifled a sob as he got in the car. Aunt Debbie came up behind Julianne and put her arms around her and kissed her cheek.

"No worries, my baby girl," Aunt Debbie said, "He'll be back in no time."

As their car pulled out of the driveway, Aunt Debbie and Uncle Charlie waved and went back inside the house. But Julianne stayed outside and watched until the car drove completely out of sight. She let out one last heart wrenching sob and then wiped the tears off of her cheeks. She sniffled and wiped her dripping nose with the tissue that Stan had supplied. She let the hot August breeze blow slowly across her face, and she closed her eyes and inhaled deeply. With Stan gone, it was time to finally put her plan into action.

Becoming Daisy

J ulianne missed Stan with every fiber of her being. She had set her plan in motion and put her conscience to rest by telling herself that what she was doing was for the both of them, for the future they would build together. For the next two weeks, Julianne worked more than ever. She worked six nights a week, and hung out with Dawn on the weekends. Dawn had become her closest confidante, and she listened intently and with sympathy as Julianne wept about the death of her sister and subsequent decline of her family.

Dawn also had a sad story; not quite as sad as Julianne's, but still sad in her own right. Dawn had never known her father, her mother had gotten pregnant with her when she was eighteen. Dawn's mother had been sleeping around, and narrowed Dawn's father down to one of twelve men, but never accused any of them of being the father. She was ninety-nine percent certain that it was the man she had met at a sit-in and slept with in the bathroom, like Dawn had said at their first meeting. Dawn grew up with her mother and a new boyfriend-of-the-month, and most of them were not very nice to Dawn. Her eyes got misty when she recalled a certain man, Paul, who had molested her at the tender age of ten while her mother was passed out drunk on the couch. Two years later, a man by the name of Don beat her and her mother so badly that they both ended up in the hospital. Dawn ran away when she was fourteen and had not seen or spoken to her mother since; she became a teenage drug addict, giving sexual favors for heroin or crack cocaine. When she was sixteen, Uncle Charlie and Aunt Debbie found her begging for change outside of a movie theater and were horrified at the sight of her bruised arms and cracked blue lips. They immediately picked her up and brought her home, bathed her, and nursed her back to health. Aunt Debbie had sat with her for days on end while she sweated, screamed, and drooled her heroin addiction right out of her body. After ten days of round-the-clock care, Dawn was cured. She had no high school education and no chance of attending college, so Uncle Charlie did the only thing he could: he offered her a job at his "company". Dawn happily accepted and had, as she put it, been Aunt Debbie and Uncle Charlie's surrogate daughter for the last fifteen years. Julianne wondered if Dawn were so close to Aunt Debbie and Uncle Charlie, why had she never met her before she started working for Charlie? She decided that some questions were better left unasked.

Julianne and Dawn bonded over their dysfunction, their career, their dreams for the future, but mostly they bonded over what they had both been missing most – a family. Their age gap was significant, but once they had established their unbreakable union, they vowed to be sisters to the end. They both had an unquestionable loyalty to each other. And, to Uncle Charlie.

When Stan came home two weeks later, he was greeted by a completely different looking Julianne. Dawn had taken her to get her hair cut and styled, and Julianne had also spent three hundred and fifty dollars of her own money on additional wardrobe. Although Stan was not unhappy with the changes, he questioned them all the same.

"I liked your hair the way it was," he protested.

Julianne giggled. "This is the style, baby."

"You know I'll love you no matter what you look like," Stan said, kissing her forehead.

"I know," Julianne said, smiling happily. Her life was perfect. She had a new best friend and pseudo-sister, a phenomenal job that made her lots of money, and an adorable boyfriend. She knew that the only thing that would make this better would be getting out of Carrollton altogether. Julianne was sometimes sad that she couldn't tell Stan about her newfound friendship with Dawn, but she knew she couldn't because Stan knew Dawn, so he would easily piece together how and why they knew each other. He worried that she was spending too much time alone, but that was because he had no idea that she spent nearly every night with a different man.

Although Julianne looked forward to Stan's visits, she also looked forward to the weekends that he wasn't home. Uncle Charlie had started booking her for two and three hour appointments, and that sometimes meant eighty or ninety dollars in one night, just for her. Julianne would come home from her appointments, fill a plastic bag with ice to sit on, and settle into her bed and count her money. She was scared that something inside her was going to rip from all the sex she was having, but when she counted nine thousand dollars in her jar one frosty night in December, the pain suddenly disappeared.

Nine thousand dollars.

Nine thousand dollars.

Julianne didn't even know what to do with one thousand dollars, let alone nine. She knew that she could probably buy a decent car, but almost wanted to save her money and get a really nice one when she could afford it. It struck her that if she spent all her money on a car then she wouldn't have any for anything else, but she also realized that there was no rush for her to leave Carrollton as long as Stan was in college and she was making thousands of dollars per year. She was content with her life and with her friendship with Dawn, so she could stay in Carrollton for another three years until Stan graduated and then the two of them could move away. Julianne calculated that she would probably have almost fifty-five thousand dollars saved up by that time, provided her hourly rate continued to go up as it had been for the past year.

The following weekend, Julianne and Dawn went out to celebrate the one year anniversary of Julianne's job. Julianne thought back to that cold December night when Richard had picked her up nearly one year ago and it seemed so far away. She was a completely different person, growing up and growing more into her alter-ego Daisy; that was for sure. She had not had a Sarah Jean nightmare in months, and her mother's impending dementia barely fazed her anymore. Under the tutelage of Dawn, Julianne had become one of Uncle Charlie's most popular girls, just as he had predicted. She was young, blonde, and full of life. Men recommended her to other men and she booked up weeks in advance. Dawn had taught her to only take on one new customer a month, because if the old customers sensed that they weren't getting enough attention, they would not come back and it would ruin Uncle Charlie's business. Julianne still saw Richard every Tuesday at the Langley Motel—and she sometimes saw two or three people after him. Uncle Charlie stopped following her to her regular appointments, like Richard and Johnny, and Julianne knew this was the ultimate sign of trust.

Every Sunday, Julianne went to Aunt Debbie and Uncle Charlie's for dinner. She dropped off her money in the bathroom and spent the rest of the evening talking to Aunt Debbie about school, and how she wanted to marry Stan when he graduated from college. Aunt Debbie would tear bridal dresses and wedding favor ideas out of magazines and save them all in a folder for Julianne. "It's never too early to start planning," she would say, "I was completely lost when Charlie proposed to me. I wish I had a folder full of ideas, it would have made my life so much easier!" The folder stayed with Aunt Debbie though, because Julianne feared what would happen if Amanda ever came across it if she should find it in her bedroom. She didn't care where she kept the folder filled with her dreams, she was just happy to have one.

As Julianne's luck would have it, her happiness was once again cut short by another Martell tragedy. Just when Julianne thought her life could not get any better, reality slapped her back down to earth.

Bob

J ulianne had just stepped off the school bus and was headed toward number 21 Senderfill on a crisp January afternoon. There was a strange car in the driveway, and alarm bells immediately went off in Julianne's head. She quickened her pace and by the time she reached the driveway, she tore up it at warp speed and flung open the front door.

Julianne saw Amanda sitting on the couch next to her mom, frantically slapping her face. "Mom! Mama! Please!" she cried. When she heard the front door slam, she turned around and saw Julianne standing perfectly still in the doorway to the living room, watching the horrific scene in front of her.

"Julianne, please help. She's not...she's not responding," Amanda sobbed. "I've been slapping her face for ten minutes. I don't think she's breathing, her lips are turning blue. Look, Julianne, they're turning fucking blue!" Tears immediately sprang to Julianne's eyes; not because her mother was comatose, but because she had not seen Amanda exhibit any kind of emotion since Sarah Jean's death. Julianne took three giant steps forward and reached the couch. She calmly sat down on the other side of her mother and pressed her two fingers up against the vein in her neck. Julianne could feel a pulse.

"She's not dead," Julianne said softly. Amanda was frantic. "How do you know? Julianne? Are you sure? What should we do?"

"Call 911. Immediately."

"Thayer!" Amanda called in the direction of her bedroom. "Thayer! Call 911! Did you hear my sister? Fucking call 911, hurry up! Mom, why aren't you answering?"

Although Julianne did not know the technical term to use for what was wrong with her mother, she gathered it had something to do with the fact that her brain was probably completely saturated with alcohol from years of drinking. Her mother had gotten up to drinking a bottle and a half of vodka a day and had been doing so for the past six months. Sandy's eyes were open, and her skin was ghostly white. Her pupils were not responsive to noise or light, but Julianne was certain she felt a pulse and could most definitely feel her mother's breath coming out of her mouth.

A dirty blond boy walked into the living room. He had bloodshot eyes and appeared to be in his early twenties. "Um, Mandy, I called 911, but…I'm gonna get the hell out of here, OK? I don't really want to be here when the ambulance gets here. This is…kind of a family thing, right?"

Amanda's face was streaked with black tears and her lips were puffy from biting them. "Go, Thayer. Thanks for calling."

"Yeah," Thayer said, and bolted out the front door ever so quickly. Julianne heard his car rev up in the driveway and zip down the street.

"Amanda, who was that?" Julianne asked. "What the hell happened here?" She was immediately angry. Just when everything was starting to go right for her, her mother was probably going to die. What would happen to her and Amanda? Would they be orphans? Would they have to leave the house?

"I was in my room with Thayer, and all of a sudden I heard this crash," Amanda said, sobbing. "Thayer and I rushed out here, and mom was just laying on the floor, really stiff and not moving. He helped me get her onto the couch and I was trying to hit her face to get her to wake up, but she wasn't answering me or moving. Then you walked in. Julianne, what's wrong with her?"

Julianne hated that just because she was calmer than Amanda at the moment, she was expected to take on the role of older sister. *Just like when Sarah Jean died,* Julianne thought. The vision of her younger self packing the family's bags and calling to purchase airline tickets burned in Julianne's mind.

Julianne shook her head and the vision disappeared. She turned to her mother, who was getting paler by the minute, and suddenly heard ambulance sirens in the distance.

"They're coming," Amanda breathed. "They're almost here, Mom. Stay with us, please, Mommy, please, please don't die!"

Julianne absentmindedly stroked her mother's hair as the wail of the sirens grew louder. Amanda's sobs also grew louder and by the time the medics busted through the front door, Amanda was in a clear state of hysteria. She blubbered and wrung her hands together as the EMT's used a penlight to look into Sandy's eyes. She began pummeling the wall with her small fists as Sandy was loaded onto the stretcher. All the while Amanda was sobbing, "Mommy, mommy, mommy, please don't leave us! Mommy, I swear I'll be good. Please, Mommy!"

Julianne stood on the other side of the room, completely removed from the situation. She felt as if she were inside of a bubble. She did not shed one tear, did not say one word as the medics wheeled her mother out of the house and tried to calm Amanda. She looked around the room, at the mementos of the house that she used to love to be in with her family, and wondered for how much longer she would see the photos of boats and flowers and deserts on the walls. She wondered for how long she would see the statue that her grandparents had gotten her parents from Italy, that was now sitting on the bookcase in the corner of the room. She wondered for how long she would notice the small hole in the corner of their tan couch, that was put there by Sandy the night she fell asleep with a cigarette in her hand and nearly burned the house down. Julianne's mind swam around and around, and she was so immersed in her own world that she almost didn't even hear the medics calling her name.

"Julianne? Julianne Martell?" a man in a blue suit said, poking her shoulder.

Julianne slowly turned her head to look at him.

"Your mom, she's going to be OK," he said soothingly. Julianne nodded slowly, unable to speak. "She's not going to die," he said.

"Thank you," Julianne finally mumbled.

"Miss Martell, do you have anyone you can call? Is there another guardian? Your sister...we're going to take her with us also, she's a little hysterical, and we want to keep her for observation to make sure she doesn't further..." his voice trailed off, but Julianne interrupted him.

"Yes, I have someone," she said crisply. She walked over to the phone and dialed Dawn's phone number. Dawn answered after the second ring.

"Dawn? It's Julianne. I, um—I'm having a bit of a family—sort of emergency—" Julianne stammered, her voice trailing off as she twirled the phone cord around her finger.

"I'll be there in ten minutes," Dawn said, and then the other line went silent.

Julianne placed the phone back into the receiver and turned to the medic. "My friend will be here in ten minutes," she said, smiling sweetly.

The medic nodded, and went back outside. Julianne went into the kitchen and poured herself a glass of water. She looked at the clock and sighed, annoyed. It was Tuesday, and Richard would be here to pick her up in about four hours. There really wasn't time for this drama today.

Julianne heard footsteps in the living room and called out, "Dawn, I'm in here."

The footsteps came toward the kitchen, and the medic who was talking to her before popped his head into the kitchen and said, "Sorry to bother you, Miss Martell. But they told me I had to stay here until someone came for you, since you're a minor."

Julianne rolled her eyes. "Fine. My friend will be here in a few minutes, and she's thirty-four, so she'll be more than glad to talk to you and let you know I'll be just fine."

"Will you be staying with her?" the medic asked.

"I don't know," Julianne was mildly irritated by all his questions. Suddenly she had a few of her own.

"Is my mother going to be OK?" she asked.

"She's not going to die," he said. "She may not be well for a while."

"Is she going to have to stay in the hospital?"

"Possibly. Probably."

"So, what happens to me and Amanda?" Julianne wanted to know.

"Well..." the medic trailed off, searching for the words. "Provided your sister is of age, and mentally capable, you should both be able to stay here. But...your sister isn't exactly....OK right now. So it will be...open for discussion."

Great, Julianne thought. *Just one more thing Amanda was going to blow.* Julianne made a mental note to go see Amanda in the hospital tomorrow (if that was in fact where they would put her) and tell her to quit the shit and get home so they could live in peace in their house for a few more years, at least.

Several moments later, Julianne heard the front door open and Dawn's familiar soprano shout, "Julianne? Honey? Where are you? What's wrong?"

"In the kitchen, D," Julianne said.

Dawn clomped into the kitchen and stopped short when she saw the medic sitting at the table. "What the fuck happened? Are you OK? Is your mother...? Where is Amanda?"

Julianne was getting sick of everyone being so damn dramatic about what was going on. As far as she was concerned, her mother brought it on herself. Julianne had been telling Sandy to stop drinking for months now and she continued to saturate her brain and her body, so Julianne had zero sympathy. "I'm fine," she said, "My mother isn't. She's not responding, so they took her to the hospital. Amanda freaked out, so they hauled her off too."

Dawn looked concerned. Especially when she saw how blasé Julianne was being about the whole thing. Julianne looked up at Dawn and said, "I have to be somewhere at seven-thirty."

Dawn looked at the medic and smiled. "I'll take it from here," she said. "I'm a family friend. She'll be staying with me until they come home, don't worry."

The medic looked utterly thankful to be relieved from his babysitting duty. He bid the girls goodbye and quickly ran out of the Martell house.

"Honey, sit down. Tell me exactly what happened," Dawn said, taking Julianne's hands in her own.

"What happened? I'll tell you what happened," Julianne said angrily. "My selfish mother, who can't think of anybody's pain but her own, finally lost her mind. She drinks all goddamn day long, not caring about my life or Mandy's life, not giving a *shit* about anyone else in this house. All that matters is her pain, her loss. Not any of ours, naturally. So she drank herself into oblivion. She probably wouldn't even bleed if you cut her, she'd probably just spurt vodka."

"Julianne...."

"I get that life is bad. It's been bad for a long time. But we all lost Daddy and Sarah Jean, not just her. She acts like it didn't affect anyone else but her. She hasn't done one motherly thing in about three years, and you know what? I just don't care anymore. She's better off in a booze coma. I'm just fine by myself," Julianne ranted.

"Do you want to stay with me tonight?" Dawn asked.

Julianne sighed loudly. "See? Constantly thinking of herself. Bet she never stopped to think what was going to happen to her other two daughters when she went nuts. Oh no, all she cared about was Sarah Jean. All she ever cared about was *fucking Sarah Jean*."

"Honey, that isn't the case. You all faced a terrible loss. You all lost Sarah Jean," Dawn tried to console her.

"I don't want to talk about it," Julianne said. "It's over, it happened. I'll stay with you tonight, after I get back from my date with Richard. Can you also drive me to the hospital tomorrow? I need to tell my sister to get her act together so we don't get kicked out of this house."

Dawn frowned, but did not argue with Julianne. "I have a date tonight myself," she said. "It'll be over by nine-thirty, so just come back here after your date and I'll be by after that to pick you up so you can sleep over. You'll be OK here by yourself until then?"

"I'll be fine," Julianne mumbled, looking at the ground. She was so angry. She needed to call Stan and get in the shower and start getting ready. She just wanted everyone to leave her alone so she could continue living her life.

Dawn gave her a hug and said, "If you need anything before I come get you tonight, you call me. Hear?"

Julianne nodded her consent and followed Dawn to the door. "Thanks, Dawn," Julianne said, attempting a smile.

"Anytime, baby," Dawn said. "You're the little sister I never had."

After she watched Dawn's car disappear down the street, she closed the door and went inside. She picked up the phone and called Stan to tell him what had happened. As predicted, Stan flipped out and wanted to leave college and come to Carrollton immediately. Julianne calmed him down, getting mildly angry that her mother and sister were the ones in the hospital, and here she was again, calming people down. Somehow, she managed to convince Stan that she was just fine.

"Where are you staying tonight?" Stan asked.

"Amanda is coming home in an hour, she called before," Julianne lied. Even after all this time, Stan was no closer to suspecting that Julianne was one of his uncle's employees and he definitely had no idea about her relationship with Dawn.

"You talked to her? Did she see your mother?" Stan asked.

"Yeah, she said mom's the same," Julianne lied again.

"Do you want to go stay at Aunt Debbie and Uncle Charlie's?" Stan asked. "Amanda can stay there too, if she wants to."

Julianne finally felt the first tug at her heartstrings that she had all afternoon. Sweet Stan. He was so good to her, and so in love with her. It was things like this that made her feel so guilty for lying to him because she really did love and care for him immensely.

"Baby, I appreciate it, but I think we both just need to be in our beds tonight," Julianne said softly. "You're sweet though, and I'll probably be over there to stay another night. Are you sure it's OK if Amanda goes too?"

"I'll talk to them but I think if I explain what's going on they'll be fine with it. She just can't pull her usual antics of coming home at six in the morning. Uncle Charlie definitely won't have that."

Julianne laughed and said, "I'm sure he wouldn't. He's no-nonsense. I'll have to let Amanda know."

She chatted on the phone with Stan for another forty minutes or so, and then bid him farewell and began her normal Tuesday night routine. She had purchased a new outfit with Dawn at the mall the previous weekend, something Richard had never seen, and she was excited to show it to him. She would be even more excited if he gave her a big tip because of her sexy new outfit.

At six-thirty on the dot, Julianne was waiting outside dutifully for Richard. But instead of Richard's car, a white Cadillac pulled up next to her. Julianne waited for him to roll the window down, but he didn't. She could just barely make out his face through the tinted windows, and could tell that it wasn't Richard. What was going on?

After sitting in the car for just about five minutes while Julianne stood outside freezing, the mystery man finally rolled the window down. Without looking at Julianne he said brusquely, "Are you getting in, or what?"

Julianne was confused by his rough manner, and was really unsure as to why Richard was not her date. She looked to the left and saw Uncle Charlie's blue Chevy parked several dozen yards away. She looked at him imploringly, hoping he would understand her confusion and give her a sign that getting in the car with this stranger was OK. As if reading her mind, Uncle Charlie stuck his hand out the window and gave Julianne a thumbs-up.

Julianne was instantly more comfortable. If Uncle Charlie was giving her the thumbs up then it must be fine. She felt a bit of a thrill go through her, she was very excited that Uncle Charlie trusted her enough to finally give her a super new customer. Julianne carefully stepped around the side of the car and opened the passenger door. The man still did not look at her, but kept his face straight ahead. Julianne stepped into the car, sat down, and shut the door. The man did not move, did not speak, and did not drive.

After what seemed like an eternity, Julianne finally figured she should say something. "I'm Daisy," she offered.

The man finally turned his head to look at her. "Bob," he sneered. "You're not that young. What are you, seventeen?"

Julianne nodded, mildly unnerved by his abruptness.

"I said I wanted someone younger. But I guess you'll do." With that, Bob put the car in drive and started moving forward slowly. In the rearview mirror, Julianne could see Uncle Charlie following her. It made her feel safe.

Bob did not say one word during the entire ride to the Langley Motel. When they got there, he appeared to know the drill, getting out of the car to get the key and leaving Julianne behind. Except while most men left the car running with the heat on, especially when it was below freezing, Bob did not. By the time he came out of the office Julianne was shivering and rubbing her hands together. Bob did not even look at her as he went to the rented room and put the key in the lock. Julianne got out of the car and followed him into the room.

Bob was nowhere to be seen when Julianne shut the hotel room door behind her. She heard a loud constant sniff coming from the bathroom and knew instantly that he was doing lines of cocaine. *Great*, she thought, *as if he wasn't already weird and mean enough.* Julianne put her purse down on the table and took off her coat. She sat down on the bed and tried to arrange herself in a sexy position.

Bob busted out of the bathroom door naked and rubbing his nose. He had no pants on and was already hard. He looked at Julianne lying down on the bed and said to her, "You're a dirty fucking slut. Do you know that? You're a DIRTY FUCKING SLUT WHORE."

Although Julianne wasn't thrilled with dirty talk, she knew how to deal with it. "Yeah, I'm your dirty little slut," she said back in a throaty, playful voice.

Bob laughed sinisterly. "No. I'm not joking around. I'm telling you – you're a dirty fucking slut. You're disgusting."

"But you're going to have sex with me anyway, aren't you?" Julianne said sweetly.

With what sounded like a snarl, Bob leapt on top of Julianne and roughly flipped her over on her stomach. He grabbed her hair and pulled it so hard it brought tears to Julianne's eyes and she whimpered softly.

"Oh, is the whore in pain?" Bob said sarcastically. Julianne did not answer. Bob, still holding Julianne's hair in a clump, pushed her face forward into the headboard. "I SAID, IS THE WHORE IN PAIN?"

The blood gushed from Julianne's nose all over the white pillows. Alarm bells went off in Julianne's head. This was not good. This was not supposed to happen. She tried to wriggle free but Bob was having none of it. "What's the matter, bitch slut?" he asked. "Don't like your job so much anymore, do you?"

"Let me go!" Julianne cried. Bob flipped her back over onto her back and whacked her across the face. Julianne tasted blood. She tried to kick with her legs but Bob was far too strong. He flipped her back over onto her stomach, ripped her panties off, and threw them on the floor. Julianne was crying hard now and begging him to stop.

"Please," she sobbed, watching her tears fall on the pillow, "I'll give you money. I'll have sex with you. I'll do whatever you want. Please stop hurting me."

"I DON'T WANT YOUR FUCKING MONEY, YOU WHORE," Bob shouted, coming close to her ear. Julianne cried harder. He shoved her head against the headboard again and Julianne saw stars. She felt vomit rise up in her throat and felt even more helpless as it came spewing out of her mouth all over the pillows. She felt like her cheekbone was broken. Bob was still holding her hair tightly in a clump, controlling her every motion. He started slapping her bare bottom so hard that it stung. She begged for him to stop.

"The whore wants me to stop, huh?" Bob said meanly.

Where the hell was Uncle Charlie?

"I wonder if the whore would like this," Bob said, spreading Julianne's legs open.

Julianne's lips were salty with her own blood and tears, and the smell of her vomit was overwhelming.

"I bet you'll like this."

Should she scream?

"Let me show you what I like."

Suddenly the pain in Julianne's rear was so intense that she could do nothing but scream at the top of her lungs. Her scream pierced the musty air in the room and she screamed and screamed so loud she felt like her voice box was going to burst. Julianne was not sure how long she lay there with the throbbing in her bottom, but thankfully it stopped and she heard Uncle Charlie's voice say, "WHAT THE MOTHER FUCK IS GOING ON IN HERE?"

Julianne put her face down in the bloody pillows, too afraid to look up. She heard Uncle Charlie shouting and the sound of a fight going on. She turned her head to look and saw Uncle Charlie give Bob a right hook that sent him sailing across the room. "WHAT DID I TELL YOU ABOUT GETTING ROUGH WITH THESE GIRLS? WHAT DID I FUCKING TELL YOU?"

Bob wiped his own nose, which Julianne noted was significantly less bloody than hers, and spit on the floor. Another man appeared in the doorway and started yelling, "Charlie, what the hell? I told you I can't have this going on here! You promised it wouldn't be messy! You better get this girl out of here immediately!"

"Take it easy, Marv," Uncle Charlie said. "I'm taking Julianne to the hospital. I'll pay for the cleanup. Get this mother fucker out of here, and don't ever allow him back."

Then Uncle Charlie turned on Bob, who was still sitting on the floor, no pants, legs spread, licking his wounds. "And you," Uncle Charlie said, more steamed than Julianne had ever seen him, "If I ever see your ugly fucking face ever again, I'll kill you. Do you understand? That's a promise. I will absolutely murder you, and dispose of the body, and no one will ever know. Do you understand me?" And with a swift kick of his sneaker, Uncle Charlie kicked Bob right between his legs.

Uncle Charlie sat down on the bed, carefully avoiding the pile of vomit, and leaned over Julianne's bloody body and whispered, "It's OK, baby. I'm going to take you to the hospital. You're going to be fine." He picked up the phone on the nightstand and dialed a number.

"Cancel your date. I need you, now. Julianne's been hurt real bad. Meet me at the hospital. You're staying with her in the emergency room."

Then he turned and gathered Julianne in his arms. He picked up her small handbag on the table and walked toward the door. Julianne turned around to look back and almost threw up all over herself again. Clumps of her blonde hair littered the sheets. The pillows were soaked with blood and there was blood on the sheets at the bottom of the bed also. Julianne felt the sting in her bottom and tears started slipping down her cheeks. The last thing she got a glimpse of before she was swept out of the room was Bob, sitting on the floor in the corner of the room, with his hand on his groin. The look in his eyes was not one of pain, however; it was a sadistic mixture of lust and hate. Julianne knew she would never forget it as long as she lived.

Try as she might, she couldn't help but wonder if the look in Bob's eyes was the last look Sarah Jean saw before her murderer killed her.

Heartbreak

In the car, Julianne's nose was still flowing blood, and Uncle Charlie grabbed a T-shirt from the back seat and put it up to her face. "I'm so sorry, Julianne," he said softly, shaking his head. "Of all my girls....I would never want this to happen to you. You're family. I never should have let you do this. I should have said no. My own stupid fault...." He kept mumbling, and Julianne wondered if he was talking to her or to himself.

Before long they pulled into the hospital, where Julianne saw Dawn's car parked in the emergency zone. Dawn pulled the door open before Uncle Charlie had even reached a full stop and started cursing and crying.

"Son of a bitch, what happened, Charlie? Oh my God, how could someone do this to her? Julianne, my honey pie, are you OK? Can you talk to me?" Dawn cried.

"Nose hurts. Ass hurts," was all Julianne could get out.

"Ass hurts? He didn't..." Dawn started, looking at Uncle Charlie.

"I don't know what happened," Uncle Charlie said, looking down, throwing his hands up in the air. "I was sitting outside and I heard her screaming, and I went to the office and got the key, we busted in and there was just blood everywhere and he was on top of her....I...I'm so sorry...."

Dawn grabbed Julianne's hand. "Can you walk, honey?" she asked. Julianne tried to nod but her head was throbbing, and the T-shirt that Uncle Charlie had given her was getting more soaked with blood by the minute. Julianne tried to put one leg out but suddenly the pain in her head was too intense and she put it back down.

"Fuck," Dawn said, turning around. She ran into the swirling emergency doors and Julianne could see her no longer. Julianne turned to look at Uncle Charlie, who was still shaking his head. She thought she could see tears in his eyes.

"Busted her whole nose," he was muttering, "Her pretty face."

Dawn came back out less than fifteen seconds later followed by two paramedics with a gurney. They came over to the car and ginger-ly pulled Julianne out and put her on the stretcher.

"You stay," Uncle Charlie directed Dawn. Dawn nodded. "I got it."

Julianne was vaguely aware of Uncle Charlie walking over to the gurney as they were strapping her in and brushing her blood-soaked hair out of her face. "I'm so sorry, my sweet baby," he choked out. He was openly crying now. Julianne's eyes fluttered and the paramedic pulled Uncle Charlie away. "We have to get her inside now," he instructed. "She's lost a lot of blood."

Dawn grabbed Julianne's hand and ran next to the stretcher as the paramedics pushed her inside the emergency door. Julianne saw white, and more white, and more white. She felt Dawn's hand contin-ue to squeeze hers as she was wheeled into a room, where several doctors in blue huddled over her and spoke in a language she

Christie Leigh Napurano

couldn't understand. They pulled the T-shirt off of her face and Julianne swore she saw one of them wince.

"Broken," one of them said. "Is she breathing OK?"

"Sweetheart," another one said, "Can you hear me? Can you breathe alright? What's her name?"

"Her name is Julianne," Julianne heard Dawn say from somewhere to her right.

"Julianne, can you breathe, sweetie?"

Julianne rolled her eyes into the back of her head and inhaled. Though it was painful, she could do it. She slowly nodded her head yes.

"OK, she's breathing," the doctor on her left said. "Get her into x-ray. I think she may have broken her cheekbone too. My God, what happened to this girl?"

"She fell down a set of stairs," Dawn said mechanically.

"How many stairs were there?" the doctor asked. Dawn didn't answer.

"We're gonna have to re-break this," one of the doctors said softly. Julianne heard him say that and her eyes opened wide and she tried to shake her head no, but the doctors were having none of it. The last thing Julianne remembered before she fainted dead away was one of the doctors coming in close to her face and the loud crack of her nose as it snapped back into place. Then everything went black.

When Julianne awoke, she was in a hospital room with an IV hooked up to her arm and a monitor beeping steadily next to her. She saw Dawn sleeping in a chair at the foot of her bed and was immediately flooded with guilt and unconditional love for her loyal friend. Julianne stirred slightly and Dawn's eyes fluttered.

⌁ 174 ⌁

"Holy shit, Julianne," Dawn said. "How are you? You had me scared half to death. And Charlie too, he's been calling every hour, he said to call him as soon as you woke up."

Julianne tried to speak, but her mouth felt like it was full of cotton. Dawn handed her a glass of water which Julianne gulped down greedily. Finally she opened her mouth to speak. "I hurt everywhere," she whispered.

"God honey, I am so sorry this happened to you. You don't even understand. Charlie is wracked with guilt. That guy was new, he actually was recommended by Richard," Dawn said. Julianne could not imagine her sweet gentle Richard associated with such a violent madman. "Richard had some business thing in the city, but he didn't want you to lose your Tuesday pay, so he sent...whoever that was."

"Bob," Julianne croaked. She would never forget his name.

"What—what happened?" Dawn asked.

Julianne took another sip of water and closed her eyes. There was Bob's leering face, licking his lips, so she quickly opened them. Her eyes filled with tears. "He—he was doing drugs," Julianne began. "So I got undressed and got on the bed. Then he just—just attacked me. Slammed my head—I threw up. I was bleeding. Oh God, did I get blood all over Uncle Charlie's car?"

Dawn shook her head. "Don't even think about it. It's fine. Our main concern is you right now."

The phone next to Julianne's bed rang and Dawn leapt to grab it. "She's awake," she said. "Talking. Not sure. See you soon."

She hung up and turned to Julianne. "Charlie and Debbie are on their way."

Julianne's eyes widened, and she winced in pain. "Debbie? What did he...?"

"The story is you fell down the stairs in your house. That's what I told the medics, that's what Charlie told Debbie and Stan, that's what we're gonna tell your mother."

Julianne had been so consumed with her own ordeal that she had completely forgotten that her mother and sister had been hospitalized not even twenty-four hours earlier. They were probably in the next room, Julianne thought bitterly. She wondered if her mother had even come out of her alcohol-induced coma yet. She sincerely doubted it.

"Stan?" Julianne asked, suddenly alarmed. "He knows?"

"Charlie told him, I think," Dawn said. "You'll have to ask him what he said when he gets here. I think he said Stan was on his way here from college though."

Julianne's head began to throb. She needed to talk to Uncle Charlie alone, before her whole secret was exposed. Aunt Debbie couldn't know what she had been doing. And Stan...God, Stan could never know. She loved Stan. She wanted to marry him. This would ruin everything. He would hate her if he found out this way, of that she was sure.

"Is my mom...?" Julianne asked Dawn.

Dawn looked at Julianne and gulped. "I knew you were going to ask that. She's two floors down, in the ICU," Dawn paused. "She hasn't...come out of it yet."

Julianne nodded. "And Amanda?"

"Checked out late last night. I called your house but no one answered."

If Julianne knew Amanda, and she was pretty sure she did, Julianne could accurately guess that Amanda was probably passed out in her man of the moment's bed. Amanda would have no idea that her younger sister almost met the same fate as her older sister just hours before, nor would she probably care.

Aunt Debbie came bursting into the room, Uncle Charlie moping behind her. "Love! Oh my Julianne, I can't believe this happened to you! My goodness they should put a gate up at the top of the stairs in your house, this is just utterly tragic!" Aunt Debbie shrieked, immediately rushing to Julianne's side and fluffing her pillows. Julianne smiled weakly. She may not have her real mother, but Aunt Debbie came in a very close second.

"How ya doin', kid," Uncle Charlie asked. Julianne could see the remorse all over his face.

"I'm ok," Julianne said. "Just really sore all over my body."

Just then Aunt Debbie noticed Dawn for the first time. "Dawn!" she exclaimed. "How on earth did you get here?" She looked suspiciously from Dawn to Uncle Charlie, then back again.

"Dawn and Julianne met a few months ago and they became friends," Uncle Charlie explained lamely. "Julianne called Dawn after she fell."

Aunt Debbie's eyes narrowed and she didn't seem to buy the explanation, but just then a nurse came into the room and shooed Aunt Debbie away from Julianne's bedside. "Just need to check your vitals," the nurse said cheerily.

Uncle Charlie, Aunt Debbie, and Dawn stood back while the nurse checked all of the machines that were hooked up to Julianne, and wrote on her clipboard. She hurried out just as quickly as she had come, waving goodbye to the visitors.

"I'm probably gonna head out," Dawn said slowly.

"Bye, Dawn. Nice seeing you," Aunt Debbie said quickly. Julianne could see that there was no love lost between the women. She wondered why, she thought Dawn was like a surrogate daughter. She would have to remember to ask....

Dawn gave Julianne a hug and whispered into her ear, "I'll be back in two hours, before my date tonight." Julianne hugged her back.

After Dawn left, Julianne attempted small talk with Uncle Charlie and Aunt Debbie. It really hurt Julianne's face when she spoke so she tried not to do it often. She hadn't seen her face yet but she gathered it was utterly hideous, not just because it ached constantly but because every new person that walked into her room winced when they saw her.

Aunt Debbie eventually excused herself to go downstairs and get a cup of coffee, and Uncle Charlie took the opportunity to talk to Julianne.

"Listen," Uncle Charlie started, "I can't apologize to you enough times. I should have done a better check on that guy, I should have reacted sooner, I shouldn't have given him to you because you're fairly new. It is all my fault and I take complete responsibility. I am going to pay for every single one of your medical bills, so don't you worry about a thing. I've already talked to the doctors."

Julianne tried to open her mouth, but Uncle Charlie silenced her, already knowing what she was going to ask. "Only Dawn knows the truth," he said. "I told Debbie and Stan that you fell down the stairs and your mom and sister weren't around so you called Dawn. Where are your mom and sister by the way?"

"My mom is...here. In the ICU."

Uncle Charlie shook his head. "Might I ask why?"

Julianne's eyes filled with tears, but because her face was numb with pain she could not feel them slipping down her cheeks. "She drank herself into oblivion," was the only way Julianne knew how to keep explaining it.

"And your sister?"

Julianne shrugged her shoulders.

"I'm going to figure out a way for you to come live with us," Uncle Charlie said. "If your sister wants to come too, we'll see what we can do. But I'm not taking no for an answer from you. And furthermore, you're done working for me."

Julianne's body started racking with silent sobs. "I want to…work," she spurted out. "I like making money. Please."

Uncle Charlie was silent for a long time. "First you get one hundred percent better, then we talk about it. Deal?" Julianne nodded. She knew she would get him to change his mind later. Julianne knew that people would probably think she was crazy but she had been thinking about her job since the minute she opened her eyes. And she didn't want to give it up. She was still young and had a few good years left in her before she was going to marry Stan, and she planned on socking away as much money as she could. There was no other job in the world that she would make the kind of cash that she had been making for the past year. Attack or no attack, she had to continue working. She would take self defense classes. She would request men who did not do drugs. She would only take clients that she had worked with before. But she would, under NO circumstances, quit her lucrative, life-changing job.

After her talk with Uncle Charlie, Julianne felt that her future was slightly more secure. She didn't necessarily want to move out of her house that she loved; but at the same time, the house was not even a home anymore, just a shell where three lonely people rattled around. The love had long since been sucked out of the house on Senderfill Road, and Julianne longed for a family, any family, similar to the one she had once known. She thought going to live with Aunt Debbie and Uncle Charlie was a wonderful idea, and she knew Stan would think so as well.

Julianne slept for the next few hours, and was unaware of Aunt Debbie and Uncle Charlie leaving and Dawn coming back. Her petite dark haired friend was sitting at the end of the bed, filing her nails, and dressed to kill when Julianne opened her eyes later that after-noon.

"You look hot," Julianne commented, smiling.

"I know. Richard tonight. He requested you, but...I wonder if he knows what his friend...." Her voice trailed off.

"Tell Richard I said hello," Julianne said softly, ignoring the rest of Dawn's comment.

Dawn and Julianne chatted and watched television for a while. They were in the middle of an intense laughing fit, Julianne crying while she laughed because it hurt her face so badly, when suddenly Dawn noticed Stan standing by the door.

"Stan!" Dawn exclaimed, straightening up immediately.

"Hi, Dawn," Stan said, quietly. He seemed confused. But before Julianne had time to analyze his reaction, his familiar tender gaze turned on her. Tears formed in his eyes as he took every inch of her injured face in. "My baby," he said, walking forward.

Stan leaned over Julianne and wrapped his entire body around her small frame. He kissed her neck, her arms, her disfigured face, while tears fell down his cheeks. "I am the worst boyfriend in the world," he whispered into her hair.

"Baby, why?" Julianne asked, pushing him away.

"I wasn't there for you," Stan said, his voice throaty. "I couldn't help you. Do you know how helpless I felt when Uncle Charlie called and told me you had fallen down the stairs and busted your entire face up? I immediately got in the car and drove here. I'm sorry it took me so long. I won't leave you ever again. I'm going to transfer colleges so I can be closer to you."

"Stan, honey, sweetie, I'm fine!" Julianne said, trying to convince him. "I'm a klutz, that's all, you know that! I'll be done with school in a few more months and then we can re-evaluate our situation. But there is no need for you to drop out of school right now! I fell down a flight of stairs, it could have happened to anyone."

Stan absentmindedly rubbed Julianne's hand as he looked deeply into her eyes. "I just want to be there for you as best I can," he said. "And you are, Stan. You really are," Julianne said. "Don't talk crazy. I'm fine!"

Stan cleared his throat and looked at Dawn, who had begun filing her nails again, pretending not to pay attention. "So, Dawn, how is it that you, um, know Julianne?"

Dawn opened her mouth and took a deep breath. Julianne beat her to the punch. "I met Dawn one day at your house, and we just clicked and became friends," she said, trying the same explanation that Uncle Charlie had given Aunt Debbie. Unfortunately, Stan was not as easy to fool as his aunt. His entire mood seemed to change as he turned on Julianne.

"Are you lying to me?" he asked Julianne, looking her square in the eyes.

Julianne felt as if the wind had been knocked out of her for the second time in less than twelve hours. "No," she lied.

"I know who Dawn is. I know what she does," Stan said. "I know her involvement with my uncle. Why are you hanging out with her?"

"Jesus, Stan, you talk about me like I'm some kind of raging slut that's not in the room. I'm right here you know, and I'm not ashamed of what I do for a living. I make more money than you ever will," Dawn said harshly.

"But why are you hanging out with my girlfriend?" Stan repeated, looking from Julianne to Dawn, searching for an answer. His tone had changed from sympathetic to sharp.

"I told you, Dawn was at your aunt and uncle's place one night when I went there for dinner," Julianne said, but she could tell that she didn't sound so sure.

Julianne saw the sickening realization hit Stan like a sucker punch in the stomach. He backed away from the bed with sudden comprehension in his eyes. "Julianne. You....couldn't. You aren't. Please tell me..." Julianne looked to Dawn, who was looking at the floor. She gulped and looked back at her boyfriend, who was now looking at her, horrified, like she was some kind of used dishrag.

"I....don't know what you're talking about, Stan," Julianne said mechanically.

"You—you're a fucking whore!" Stan sputtered. "You're working for my uncle, aren't you? Oh my God. Oh my God. This is impossible." He frantically paced back and forth around her bed, running his hands through his hair and then leaning up against the wall for support.

Dawn stood up and quietly slipped out of the room, giving Julianne and Stan their privacy.

"I was going to make you my wife. I loved you, Julianne. How could you betray me like this?" The pain in Stan's voice was evident. She could see the heartbreak all over his face.

Julianne's throat was raw, but she tried to talk anyway. She was caught. She knew she had to confess. She only hoped that she could convince Stan to see it her way. She hoped she could convince him not to leave her. "Stan—you don't understand," she began.

He cut her off. "Understand? Understand? Oh, I understand all right. You come into my life, and you're perfect. I fall madly in love with you and make you part of my family. Then you go behind my back and work for my uncle – a pimp – and *fuck* other men? Do you understand how completely devastating that is to me? Julianne, do you?"

Julianne sniffled and wiped the tears from her eyes. "Stan, listen to me....I had no choice. I have to get out of here. I have to get out of Carrollton," she sobbed. "My life is falling apart. My sister is dead. My father is gone. My mother—my mother is in a room somewhere in this hospital with a nonfunctioning brain. What choice did I have?" There was a deafening roar in Julianne's ears as she could tell Stan wasn't buying it.

"I needed to make money to get out, and unfortunately, Seth's Ice Cream just wasn't cutting it anymore," she said bitterly. "So forgive me for wanting to better my life. I had to make enough money to get out of this town. But I was doing it for us! I was doing it for our future! I wasn't going to leave you, I swear. I was just going to do it long enough to make enough money so that we could be happy. Stan, please..."

Stan shook his head and held his hands out. He didn't want to hear another word. With tears in his eyes he looked at Julianne and asked the words she had hoped he wouldn't. "How long?"

Julianne shook her head. "It's not important, I—"

"How long, Julianne?"

Julianne put her head down and said meekly, "A little over a year."

"Holy shit," Stan cursed, punching the wall. "You've been fucking men every night while I'm gone for over a year? Julianne, how could you *do* this to me? How could my uncle do this to me?"

Stan collapsed into the chair at the end of the bed, putting his head in his hands and rubbing his temples. "I'm sorry," Julianne sobbed. "I hated lying to you." She hated to sound so trite, but it was the truth, after all.

It seemed like they sat there for an eternity; Julianne, sniffling and rubbing her eyes and swallowing painfully, and Stan, staring at the floor while he wrung his hands methodically. Finally, he looked up.

"Julianne, I cannot in good faith continue a relationship with you."

"Stan—"

"No. There are no more conversations to be had. There is nothing else to say," Stan whispered ruefully. "I don't want to see you, or my Uncle Charlie, ever again."

Julianne began openly sobbing. "Stan, please. I love you. Please. You can't do this to me. I almost died. I need you. I—"

"You put yourself in that position," Stan barked with a hardness she had never heard. "I feel no sympathy. You wanted this life....you got it."

Stan stood up and looked at Julianne one last time. "I sure hope you make enough money to do whatever it is that was so much more important to you than I ever was," he said, his voice hoarse with emotion. And before Julianne had time to say anything else, he walked out the door.

"STAN!" Julianne shouted after him. She was not going to let him walk away. He was her future. He was half of her ticket out of Carroll-ton. She mustered up all the strength she could and tried to pull herself out of the bed. The monitors started beeping rapidly as she pulled tubes and needles out of her body and stood up on the cold, hard hospital floor. "STAN!" she called again, her voice breaking. She began to go after him but a flash of something to her left caught her eye and she took a painful step backwards.

Her reflection in the mirror.

Another New Life

Julianne was a monster. She didn't know how people had come and gone in this room all day and been able to stomach the sight of her. There was a sewn up gash on her right cheek that was crusted over with dried blood. The bruises under her eyes were a shade of purple Julianne had never seen before, mixed in with blues, yellows and greens. Her nose was swollen to twice its normal size, having been broken twice. She had random scratches on her forehead and chin, and another cut just above her right eye that was oozing some sort of whitish bodily fluid. She gasped in horror and her hand immediately flew to her face, as if she didn't believe it were her own. Sure enough, she felt the stitches in her cheek, the tenderness of her nose, and finally, wiped the pus from the cut above her eye. Lifting her upper lip, Julianne finally realized why her gums hurt so much. There was an enormous frightening scratch above her two front teeth.

Julianne's own reflection in the mirror was so shocking that she almost forgot why she had gotten up in the first place. Julianne started calling out Stan's name and dry heaving as she collapsed to the floor. Not a moment later, two nurses came in and put her back in bed and hooked her back up to her monitors.

Julianne spent a very lonely afternoon and evening by herself. She slept fitfully, Bob's ghoulish stare and Stan's heartbroken face haunting her every time she closed her eyes. The only people she saw were the nurses as they came in and out every few hours to check on her and change her fluids and bandages. Julianne longed for the Sarah Jean nightmares; they were peaceful in comparison to the torture she was experiencing now. She had lost Stan. Her heart felt as if it had been torn in two pieces as she wept bitterly and scolded herself for her poor decisions. She should have just stuck it out in her miserable house for another year until she was done with school and then she could have moved to New Jersey and been with Stan. That would never happen now. She wondered if Uncle Charlie and Aunt Debbie were going to abandon her now as well, then she would surely be an orphan. The thought alone made her head swirl.

The next morning came and went with no sign of any visitors. Julianne started to weigh her options as far as where she would go when she felt well enough to check out. She would need to hitchhike a ride back to her house; that was for certain. Not only was her money there, but she wanted to at least pack as much stuff as she could carry if she were going to leave. She thought she might be able to stay with Dawn for a while, but figured it might be best if she just cut everyone out from her old life altogether. Julianne wondered where she could go that wouldn't be expensive and what she could do without a high school diploma that would earn her enough to live comfortably.

Just as Julianne started dozing while making a mental list of things in the house she could pawn off for money, she heard Uncle Charlie and Dawn speaking in hushed tones outside the doorway.

"Do you think she's gonna tell anyone?" she heard Uncle Charlie whisper.

"No, I really don't," Dawn whispered back, "But you can never tell. Poor thing is so desperate for money she might do anything for a buck, even if it means turning us in. I don't like to think that about her, I like to think she thinks of us like family, but you know me. Always the pessimist."

Julianne was slightly shocked to hear that Uncle Charlie and Dawn would think that she would betray them. She vowed that she would not, seeing as Dawn was right—they were her family.

Uncle Charlie and Dawn stopped talking and appeared in the doorway of her hospital room. Julianne immediately forgot the conversation she had just overheard them having, and was overcome with emotion at the sight of them. She started crying, and Dawn rushed toward her and embraced her. "I'm so sorry about yesterday, Julianne," Dawn said. "Me too," Julianne echoed.

Uncle Charlie cleared his throat and Dawn let go of Julianne.

"Many things have happened over the last forty-eight hours," Uncle Charlie began, "That already have and could continue to be detrimental to many people. We are now going to have to go into cleanup mode, and seeing as you two are my most trusted and most involved, you will become part of the plan."

Julianne nodded, and Dawn obediently took a seat. Uncle Charlie continued.

"First order of business is Debbie. She…found out about you, Julianne. When Stan called…."

Julianne gasped. What must Aunt Debbie think?

"She's not mad at you," Uncle Charlie said, as if reading Julianne's mind. "She's more angry at me. Thinks I conned you into it. Of course I didn't tell her that you begged me, I let you maintain your innocence, in her eyes." Uncle Charlie winked. Dawn chuckled softly.

"Debbie has agreed to let you come and live with us when you are released, under the premise that you will not continue to work for me, and that you will adhere to rules and a schedule under our roof. She doesn't want you to ever talk about my job or the fact that you ever worked for me. She also doesn't want you to see Dawn anymore."

Julianne looked at Dawn, alarmed. Tears began to form in Dawn's eyes. "Charlie, I love this girl...she's like the sister I never had."

"Listen," Charlie said gruffly, "Unless the two of you want to go live hungry on the streets together, these are the rules. Of course, me and Debbie aren't gonna be keeping an eye on you every second of every day, Julianne. What you do with your own personal time is none of our business, you catch my drift?"

Julianne did. She nodded silently, afraid to speak.

"Second of all, Stan."

Julianne's heart ached at his name.

"Stan came over to the house yesterday like a crazy person, after he left here. Of course I knew he was coming because Dawn had called me and told me what had happened and what he had found out. Julianne, I truly am sorry. He has completely written me and Aunt Debbie off as family, says he never wants to see either one of us again, and—-he says he never wants to see you again either. Of course that may all change once he cools off, so let's not jump to conclusions just yet."

Julianne bit down hard on her lip to keep from crying. She knew from the way that Stan looked at her yesterday that he would never cool down. He had loved her and she broke his heart. She knew deep down in her soul that she would probably never see Stan again in her lifetime.

"Third. Julianne, when you are released from here, we're gonna...do you over. Fix you up a bit."

"Makeover," Dawn explained.

"Right, makeover, whatever you call it," Charlie continued. "Dawn will check you out when it's time and bring you to a salon. You're gonna get a whole new hair color and new hairdo. Got it? I want *no one* recognizing you," Charlie instructed.

Julianne nodded again. She didn't want a makeover, but she didn't have much in the way of options at the moment. She reminded herself that she was going to do whatever it took to prove to Uncle Charlie that she would not betray him, so it was either Charlie's way or the highway...literally.

"If you are going to be living under my roof as my and Debbie's daughter, I don't want anyone to even suspect that you might have done what you used to do. Debbie won't have it, and neither will I. Lastly," Uncle Charlie said with finality, "You do not have to worry about Bob ever again. He won't find you, he won't bother you. If we're lucky, he won't be found himself."

Uncle Charlie chuckled sadistically, and Julianne felt dizzy. Did that mean he had Bob killed? Was Uncle Charlie a pimp, and a killer? And she had just agreed to move in with him....

Dawn's twinkling voice suddenly pulled Julianne back to reality. "So...that's the plan, Julianne! Got any questions?"

A million, Julianne thought, but she shook her head quickly and plastered a smile on her still pained face. "You look better today," Uncle Charlie complimented her. "Thank you," she returned.

"Alright, well, I'm gonna head out of here," Uncle Charlie said. "Debbie will be by in the morning, Julianne. She said to tell you hello but she just needed a day to process everything, alright? She doesn't hate you, I promise." He walked over to Julianne's bedside and kissed the top of her head. "See you soon, kiddo. If you need anything, just call."

After Julianne was sure he was safely down the hall and out of earshot, she pounced on Dawn for information. "I lied," she said brazenly. "I have a few questions."

Dawn grinned. "Thought you might," she said.

"First of all," Julianne said, imitating Uncle Charlie. Dawn giggled. "First of all, is it really true that we can't be friends?"

Dawn blew a raspberry with her lips and waved her perfectly manicured hand. "No way, you ain't gettin' rid of me that easily, honey. You heard Charlie. They can't monitor you 24/7. We'll have plenty of hangout time, don't you worry. By the way, I think now that you have all that money saved up and nowhere to go, it's time we got you a license…and a flashy car to drive."

Julianne smiled and her spirits started to perk up. Maybe this life wouldn't be so bad after all.

"What else you got?" Dawn asked.

"I don't even want to ask about Stan," Julianne said sadly.

"Nothing to tell," Dawn said shortly. "I wish there was. Like Charlie said, after I left the room yesterday I called him and told him that Stan was here going off on you because he saw me and figured everything out. Then I guess he went over there, threw a few things around, and yelled at Uncle Charlie until he popped a blood vessel in his face, and left. That's all I know."

Julianne closed her eyes and felt her chest ache with longing. She was so terribly sad that she had caused Stan so much pain and wished she could see him just one more time to tell him exactly that.

"I know you're upset about him, Julianne. I'm not going to tell you to get over it, though. You're allowed to mourn. He meant a lot to you. But listen, now that you're straight and not working anymore you can find someone else who will love you just as much, and who will never have to know," Dawn said.

She was right, Julianne reasoned. Still, she knew she would probably never love anyone the way she loved Stan. She sighed, her heart heavy, but pressed on with her queries.

"I have two more questions," Julianne said, not wanting to lose momentum.

"Go," said Dawn.

"Why do Aunt Debbie and Stan hate you?"

"What makes you say that?"

"Dawn, I saw the way they looked at you when they came in here. Obviously Aunt Debbie knows you and Stan knows what you do, but there seems to be something else going on."

Dawn pursed her lips and let her breath out in a whoosh. "Charlie and I...dated. Back in the day," she said.

"That's it?" Julianne asked.

"Not exactly," Dawn said. "After Debbie and Charlie took me in, and I got clean, I was staying with them for a while. Just until I could save up enough money to get my own place, ya know? One night

Debbie was out, I came home from a date, Charlie was drunk, and um, you can guess the rest. Debbie found us in their bed. She almost killed me that night. Charlie had to pull her off of me. I had bruises on my neck for days, she choked the shit out of me so bad."

Julianne was aghast. She could not picture Dawn having sex with Uncle Charlie, and she most definitely could not see Aunt Debbie getting violent with someone.

"I got my own place the next day. Charlie paid for it until I could afford it myself. We never touched each other again, but Debbie doesn't believe that. She doesn't like that he and I are such good friends. She definitely doesn't like that I work for him, but what is she really gonna say? I mean, indirectly, I pay for her fancy jewelry, her manicures, and her fake tits. She knows I'm one of the top girls and that I make her husband tons of money. She knows that if I go, her weekly massage might go too. So, she deals. She doesn't like me, but she deals," Dawn said matter-of-factly.

"Wow," Julianne said. She wondered to herself why Dawn had lied to her when she first asked last year if there had ever been anything between her and Uncle Charlie. She hoped that Aunt Debbie didn't think that she, Julianne Martell, would ever be capable of such a thing, especially now that she was going to be living under their roof like Dawn had been.

"You never tell a soul that I told you that, got it?"

"Of course not. Does Stan know? Is that why he doesn't like you either?"

"Yeah," Dawn nodded. "OK, enough of that. What was the last question?"

Julianne shook her head, still trying to take in what Dawn had told her, but she couldn't lose focus. "What did Uncle Charlie mean...about Bob...when he said that he would never bother me again?"

"You caught that, huh," Dawn said. "Charlie's too nonchalant for his own good."

Julianne looked at her expectantly.

"Bob's gone. He's left this Earth as we know it. He ain't here walking around with us anymore, so you'll never see him again. Follow?" Dawn said.

"He's—-dead?"

Dawn raised her eyebrows and her mouth dropped open a little in mock surprise. "Don't look so shocked there, honey. You've seen the ugly side of this business first hand. Now you know how truly ugly it can get."

"Why?" Julianne couldn't believe that Uncle Charlie had killed someone.

"He'll talk," Dawn explained. "Talk to cops, talk to other clients, who will think they can treat us like shit and get away with it. So now he isn't talking to anyone, except the other bodies at the bottom of the Hudson."

"Did...Uncle Charlie do it?"

Dawn laughed. "Of course not. He would never do it himself. He calls someone, who calls someone, who does it. Charlie's a pimp— he's not a killer."

This made Julianne slightly more comfortable, but only slightly. The fact that Uncle Charlie could end someone's life with a simple phone call was profound. Dawn could see Julianne getting uptight and she stood up and walked over to her bedside. "We don't talk about that shit, though, Julianne, OK? You don't know that. Do you hear me? Unless you want to put me and Charlie behind bars, you *never* mention it again. I need to hear you say you understand me."

Dawn was scaring her, so Julianne agreed. She had always known that Dawn was fiercely loyal to Uncle Charlie, but now she was talking about being an accomplice or an accessory to murder. And in Julianne knowing this information, she realized that it made her one as well.

"I got it," Julianne said. "I promise."

Dawn made her pinky swear, and then she seemed satisfied, so she went and sat back down. "So what color you think you're gonna dye your hair?"

"I don't really want to dye it," Julianne said softly, grabbing a wisp of her blonde hair absentmindedly.

"You have to," Dawn said. "It's not really an option, Julianne. If Charlie says to do it, you do it. Do you understand how lucky you are right now? Because I don't think you do. Charlie and Debbie are taking you in. They're taking you in as one of their own, because they care about you. Otherwise who knows what would happen to you?"

Though Julianne didn't like that Dawn was getting a bit snippy with her, Julianne realized that she did have a point. Uncle Charlie and Aunt Debbie didn't have to take her in, especially after what Aunt Debbie had found out. They were doing it because they were good people. And the last thing that Julianne wanted to do was irritate the people who were going to put a roof over her head and food in her stomach.

"I don't want to go too dark," Julianne said. "Do you think I could just do it a light brown?"

"Of course," Dawn replied, "As long as it's noticeably different. Charlie just doesn't want any old clients to recognize you for a while, that's all. It'll grow out in a few months and then it'll be blonde again."

Julianne didn't dare say it, but the reason she wanted to keep her hair blonde was in honor of Sarah Jean. She liked resembling her and felt that changing her hair would make the memory of her sister fade away. But, she rationalized; a few months with brown hair wouldn't hurt.

After three days of laying in her hospital bed, her only visitors being Uncle Charlie, Aunt Debbie, and Dawn, Julianne got bored and decided to take a walk around the hospital one morning. She was given permission by her doctor to walk around; the nurses said it might even be good for her. She had to use a walker, but she didn't care. She was thrilled to be out of that room, even if it was only temporarily.

She knew exactly where she was going before she even got there. As she turned the corner, the name of the unit taunted her in big white and blue letters above the door.

INTENSIVE CARE.

Julianne pushed through the doors and hobbled down the hallway on her walker. She slowly and cautiously peered into every room, seeing cancer patients and old men and women suffering from Alzheimer's and other aging diseases. Finally, at the very end of the hall, Julianne found what she was looking for.

Sandy had the only single room in the entire unit. Julianne wondered why that was. She shuffled into the room, careful not to slip on the impeccable linoleum floor, and right up to the foot of her mother's bed. She picked up the clipboard with her mother's charts, and though she could barely read the doctors' scribble, she understood three terms: *alcohol, brain damage,* and *unresponsive.*

Tears filled Julianne's eyes as she put the cold metal clipboard back into its slot at the end of the bed. She disengaged herself from the walker, and putting her hands on the bed and her weight on her hands, she made her way around the side of the bed and stared at her mother.

Even in her expressionless state, Sandy Martell was flawless. Her blonde hair which had become streaked with grey over the past several years was flayed out on the white pillows. Her skin was like porcelain, even more so because she had been involuntarily detoxed over the past few days, so the toxins were leaving her body and her face was no longer red and bloated. She was not breathing on her own, but with the help of a machine. Her eyes were slightly open, just enough so that Julianne could see their sky blue color peeking through. There was no life in them though, and that made Julianne start to sob. She crawled into bed with her mother, put her arms around Sandy, and heaved great wracking sobs into her chest. For what seemed like the millionth time, Julianne asked herself how this could have happened. How did an entire family unravel and simply fall apart in a matter of three years? And last but not least, where the hell was Amanda?

Julianne lay in bed with her mother for what seemed like hours, crying and apologizing and rubbing Sandy's hands and arms. She thought maybe that if her mother heard her voice she would come out of her coma, but after painstaking hours of talking and touching she realized it was to no avail. Sandy Martell was gone. Not physically, but for all intents and purposes, she was no longer there. Admitting that simple fact to herself made Julianne break down into tears again, and she felt the same anger toward her mother that she felt toward Sarah Jean. How could Sandy have been so stupid to think that there would not be consequences for her selfish actions? Did she really care that little about Julianne and Amanda that she actually tried to drink herself to death? In a sudden moment of passion, Julianne sat up and slapped her mother across the face.

"How could you?" she sobbed. "I'm all alone, mother. I'm all alone! It isn't fair! I'm seventeen years old and all alone…." And then, consumed with her own self pity, she fell back into her mother's soft, warm torso again.

After Julianne had cried all the tears she could possibly cry, she bid a final farewell to her mother and shuffled back out the door just as quietly as she had come in. She would not be back to see Sandy, as far as she was concerned that was their final goodbye. She knew that Sandy had no other relatives to speak for her, and that if no one came forward to make a decision about her mother then they would just pull the plug eventually. Julianne did not want to be around for that, although she was sure she would read about it in the papers.

The Final Nail

F or the next few days, Julianne tried not to think about her mother or sister, but rather focus on the transition of becoming the responsibility of Uncle Charlie and Aunt Debbie. Every time either one of them came to see her, they expressed how truly excited they were for her to move in, and she finally felt something that had been missing from her life for many years: feeling wanted.

Before long Julianne's face had just about healed, her black eyes had just slight shades of blue left, and her nose was not excruciatingly painful to the touch. She was ready to go home. Uncle Charlie and Aunt Debbie showed up, with a teddy bear and balloons. Julianne's eyes filled with tears and she once again thought how lucky she was to finally be part of a family again.

Julianne spent the next several days with Aunt Debbie. They went shopping for new clothes, and Julianne got her hair dyed a light shade of brown. Looking in the mirror after it was done, she decided she looked a little more like Aunt Debbie with this color and thought that maybe, just maybe, she could get used to it. The more time she spent with Charlie and Debbie, the more Julianne thought that it was time to let go of her old life. So she asked Aunt Debbie if she would do her just one more favor before she legally changed her name to Julianne Delgando; she asked her to take her back to 21 Senderfill.

Aunt Debbie was only too happy to oblige, but on the terms that she would enter the house with Julianne and that Julianne was not allowed to be alone in any part of the house at any time. Julianne agreed to the terms. There were things in her room that she wanted. Most of all, she wanted that money under her bed.

A sense of dread and fear enveloped Julianne as they made the turn onto Senderfill Road. Her house looked haunted; one of the two lights on either side of the front door had been broken, and there was a hole in the latticework on the front porch. Leaves were strewn over the welcome mat, and the front screen storm door banged softly against the frame, the latch obviously broken.

"Good thing we came when it was light out!" Debbie said cheerily. Julianne tried not to be so depressed about the ruins of her once-thriving home. Her heart ached with emptiness and longing and she sniffled, unable to take her eyes off the house. Aunt Debbie turned to her with concern. "Oh, Julianne, honey, we don't have to do this! Should we go home? Let's do it another day."

Julianne shook her head adamantly. They were there, she wanted to just get it over with and then never come back to this part of town again. Most of all, she wanted to check for any sign of Amanda.

The women got out of the car and walked towards the house. Julianne walked boldly up the steps and grabbed the storm door before it could slam against the frame again, and pulled it open. She turned the doorknob, and the door opened easily. It had been left unlocked.

There was an eerie sense of calm inside the house. Everything looked just as Julianne had left it on the night she had been attacked. There was a thin layer of dust over most things, but Julianne realized that it had been there before. Sandy hadn't lifted a finger to clean the house in months. They walked down the hallway towards the kitchen and Aunt Debbie accidentally kicked a glass tumbler that was lying on the floor. The noise startled Julianne and she jumped, but she knelt down to pick up the glass. The kitchen was untouched, the living room was untouched, and the bathroom was untouched.

"It doesn't look like my sister has been back here," Julianne whispered to Aunt Debbie, who nodded in response.

They made their way toward the stairs. Aunt Debbie and Uncle Charlie had promised to buy her everything new that she needed for her bedroom, but there were a few irreplaceable things that she wanted from her old bedroom. And from Sarah Jean's.

Julianne walked by Sarah Jean's closed bedroom door, and went straight to Amanda's room at the end of the hall. Aunt Debbie followed in silence, sensing that it was not her place to say anything. Julianne pushed open Amanda's creaky door, and to her dismay the bedroom looked just like the rest of the house – completely untouched. Julianne flung open Amanda's closet and saw that most of her clothes were missing. *So she had been back*, Julianne thought. Suddenly an icy dread clutched at Julianne's heart, and she busted past Aunt Debbie back down the hallway into her own bedroom.

It was ransacked. Just as Julianne had suspected.

Her clothes were all over the room, her mattress had been pulled off the bedframe and was lying on the floor, her curtains had been torn down. Julianne's throat began to close as she surveyed the room and her eyes fell on the glass jar that held the ten thousand dollars she had saved up....and it was completely empty.

A loud wail rose up from Julianne's throat and her heart pounded in her ears. "NOOOOOOOOOOOOOO!" she yelled. Amanda had come back. Amanda had come back and stolen her money and left. Amanda had betrayed her, had stabbed her in the heart one final time before running off. Julianne collapsed on the floor, hyperventilating. Aunt Debbie rushed into the room and sat on the floor with Julianne as she coughed and sobbed, and rubbed her back.

"Honey, what's missing?" Aunt Debbie asked, completely unaware.

"My money," Julianne choked out. "My money. It's gone. I had ten thousand dollars. She took it. She took it and she's never coming back."

Aunt Debbie's eyes narrowed quickly, because she knew how Julianne had made that money, but her heart went out to the girl. Debbie had a shitty sister, but her sister would never steal ten thousand dollars from her, that was for sure. She sat there with Julianne in hysterics, unsure of what to do.

Finally after Julianne had wailed for a good fifteen minutes, Aunt Debbie said, "Sweetie, I think it's time to leave. Is there anything else here that you want? Come on, it's not good for you to be here, I don't think..."

Julianne picked herself up off the floor and walked out of her room without touching a thing. She had two dead sisters, a dead mother, and a dead father. She was truly alone. But then she felt Aunt Debbie's hand on her shoulder and a sense of comfort came over her. She marched back down the hallway, stopping in front of Sarah

Jean's door. Pushing it open, she strode into the room quickly and picked up the picture frame that sat on Sarah Jean's desk. The picture of Julianne and Sarah Jean that had been taken just before she went to college. Julianne would treasure it always.

As for the rest of the stuff in the house, Julianne wished she could find someone to burn it down.

Julianne felt no emotion as she and Aunt Debbie walked out of the broken down house and got into the warm car. Once she had fastened her seatbelt, she turned to Aunt Debbie, and said only, "Thank you." Aunt Debbie nodded, and they did not speak another word for the remainder of the car ride.

When they got home, Aunt Debbie started dinner and they watched television while they waited for Uncle Charlie. When Julianne heard his key turn in the front lock, she felt a sense of ex-citement...the same sense of excitement she used to feel when she heard her father's key as he was returning home from a day's work. Charlie smiled as he stepped into the living room and looked at his girls.

"How was your day? What did you guys—" Uncle Charlie started to ask, but Aunt Debbie widened her eyes and shook her head and he clammed up. Instead, he looked at Julianne and said, "I love your hair, honey! It looks wonderful. You look even prettier than you used to." Julianne smiled and took the compliment.

The next week passed uneventfully. Julianne did not want to re-turn to school, she didn't feel she was ready yet. Between the attack, the complete loss of her remaining family members, and the devastat-ing end of her and Stan's relationship, she felt more comfortable getting home schooled by Aunt Debbie, and her new guardians agreed. Julianne had taken one of the three bedrooms in the house, Aunt Debbie had set the smallest one up like a classroom, complete with a desk, a chalkboard, and a bookcase with all the school text-books Julianne had used in school. Julianne was rarely without Debbie or Charlie, and she didn't mind the constant company. She still went for her daily run, carefully avoiding her old path, and it was the only solitary hour she had per day. She thought maybe after the summer she could get a job, since she had decided to take the year off before she started applying to colleges, and she was hoping to broach the subject with Uncle Charlie and Aunt Debbie soon. But right now she wanted to concentrate on finishing her studies and getting her GED. The Delgandos had filed a petition to make themselves her legal guardian and accordingly, changed her last name; and the papers were due to come in the following week. Julianne could not wait to officially become Julianne Delgando and leave Julianne Martell far, far behind.

Once again, she was at a point in her life where she could see happiness approaching, and that's when she saw the newscast that she had been dreading.

A Glimmer of Hope

J ulianne was helping Aunt Debbie make dinner in the kitchen, and the television had been left on in the family room. Just as she had put a pan of marinated chicken in the oven, she heard the voice of a female newscaster say, "…doctors at Long Island Hospital South made the decision to take Martell off of life support today, as she had been in the hospital for nearly two months with no visitors, and no family to speak for her."

Hearing her last name sent shock waves through her, and she looked at Aunt Debbie to see if she had heard, but the smile on Aunt Debbie's face told her she hadn't.

"I have to use the bathroom," Julianne whispered numbly, and she crept slowly into the living room to stand behind the couch and watch the horror on the box in front of her.

"Sandra Martell had been brought into the hospital nearly two months ago following an incident at her Carrollton home. Her nineteen-year-old daughter Amanda was brought in with her, but was released the following day. There has been no sign of Amanda since her release. Officials say that Martell's other daughter Julianne was admitted to the hospital the same day as well, but there has been no sign of her in weeks either," said the pretty young brunette reporter, who was standing in front of the hospital where Julianne had stayed just weeks ago. She was holding a microphone and had a concerned expression on her perfectly painted face. Julianne instantly hated her.

Showing no mercy, the reporter continued. "The Martell family made headlines two years ago when their eldest daughter, Sarah Jean, was found murdered at a small college in Vermont. Early sometime last year, the head of the household Alan Martell, became estranged from the family and was found burglarizing a small store several towns over. He was jailed but released, and there has been no sign of him since." As the reporter spoke, photos of Sarah Jean and Alan flashed across the screen. Julianne felt her entire body go completely numb as she stared into the faces of her beloved family.

"Today, the unresponsive Sandra Martell was taken off of life support. Authorities have tried to get in touch with any family members, but aside from Martell's two remaining daughters, most are deceased. Officials have searched the residence where the family resided on Senderfill Road but found nothing."

At this point, footage of the decrepit Martell household flashed onto the screen. Several policemen were shown entering the house, guns drawn. Julianne saw the front storm door banging methodically in the wind and felt a sudden urge to tear it right off the hinges.

"The whereabouts of Sandy Martell's two remaining daughters, Julianne and Amanda, remain unknown."

Julianne was shocked to see a photo of her, Amanda, and Sarah Jean pasted on the television, with her and Amanda's faces highlighted.

"If you have any information about the mysterious disappearance of these two girls, please call our tip line at 1-800-WNRC-TIP. This is Martha Jacobs, reporting for WNRC News."

The anchors began chirping the next story, but Julianne's mind stayed fixed on what she had just heard. Authorities were looking for her and Amanda? She knew why they hadn't found her, but where the hell was Amanda?

Spending all your hard earned money, said a voice in Julianne's head. It was hard not to be bitter about the fact that Amanda had stolen all of the money Julianne had made to escape, and it hurt even more that she had probably spent it all on drugs. Though sometimes Julianne wished that Amanda would fall into harm's way, she also sometimes thought about asking Aunt Debbie and Uncle Charlie to help her find her sister. Then her thoughts would once again circle back to the stolen money, and she would decide against it. She had a good life here, and bringing Amanda into it would only cause chaos, of this Julianne was sure.

After regaining her composure, Julianne went into the bathroom and washed her face. Then she went back into the kitchen, her face showing no emotion, and she set the table for dinner.

Months passed, and the end of Julianne's "school year" was approaching. It was late June, and Julianne had taken to the Delgandos' as if she had always lived there. On occasion she thought about her family, but she never spoke of them. More often than not her thoughts fell on Stan, and she wondered how he was doing. She would never ask Uncle Charlie and Aunt Debbie if they had heard from him or his parents, but she was pretty sure that they hadn't. After all, she was with Debbie most of the day, so she would probably know. Her heart longed for him and she wondered if she would ever find anyone who cared for her and all of her idiosyncrasies and insanity the way Stan did. There were many times when she considered calling him, but she would always lose her nerve and walk away from the phone. Sometimes she stood by the phone and stared at it, willing it to ring, praying he would hear her telepathic pleas. But there was never anything. Though Julianne doubted it very much, she prayed nightly that she would one day get to see Stan to at least apologize.

Five days a week Julianne went for her run. Three of those days, she would meet Dawn at the end of the street. They would go for lunch, or walk around the mall for a bit, and Dawn always treated her to a sandwich or a soda. Julianne told Dawn about the newscast she had seen about her family, and while Dawn expressed sympathy, she tried to assuage Julianne's grief and help her focus on all of the positive things in her life and what was coming up in the future. Dawn was the only person she could talk about her family with. For some reason she felt guilty mentioning them in front of Aunt Debbie and Uncle Charlie, almost as if she were betraying them because they were her "new family". And though Julianne tried to ask Dawn questions about work, or her old clients, Dawn would not answer and would steer the conversation in a completely different direction. Julianne couldn't be certain, but she figured Uncle Charlie had told Dawn not to discuss it with her. Because their friendship had a time limit, it was not the same as it had been before, but Julianne was grateful for Dawn's continuing support and love toward her.

Late one night, Julianne got out of her plush bed and began walking down the hallway toward the bathroom. She overheard hushed voices talking in the master bedroom and paused at Charlie and

Debbie's door to try and listen to their conversation, but all she caught were bits and pieces.

"....looks completely different...."

"....happy here, should we...."

"....can barely tell she's the same person she was...."

"....really necessary, I've grown to care..."

Julianne strained to hear the exchange better and took a step closer to the door. A loud creak erupted from the old floorboards, and Julianne stepped backward in alarm and continued walking toward the bathroom so as not to be caught. She knew they were talking about her, but what were they saying? It sounded like they were talking about her progress and were wondering if she was happy there. She decided she would make it a point the next morning to tell them how thankful she truly was.

"I know I've said it before," Julianne said at breakfast the next morning, "But, I just want to say thank you again so much for taking me in. I really owe the two of you, I don't know where I would have gone or what I would have done without you. I'm very happy here and I love you both."

Aunt Debbie and Uncle Charlie exchanged glances, and Aunt Debbie looked down at the table. Uncle Charlie took a deep breath.

"Julianne," he began, "There's something we need to talk to you about."

Julianne immediately stiffened. Were they kicking her out? But Uncle Charlie said something that Julianne was completely unprepared for.

"Stan called."

Julianne nearly choked on her blueberry pancakes and had to take a swig of milk before she finally sputtered, "When?"

"Yesterday," Aunt Debbie said. "While you were out for your run."

Julianne's mind raced. "What did he say?"

"He said—he said he wanted to see you," Uncle Charlie said.

"He does?" Julianne was incredulous. She had dreamed of this chance, but had not dreamed it would come so soon.

"He's home for the summer," Uncle Charlie continued, "Living at home and working, out by Hackettstown. He doesn't want to come back here, he says he isn't ready, but he asked if I could drive you out there so you two could meet."

Julianne didn't know what to say. Losing her entire family and Stan in one blow had been almost as devastating as losing Sarah Jean, but if she could at least have one of them back....

"When can we go?" she asked, all smiles.

Uncle Charlie cleared his throat and hesitated before answering, "Tomorrow."

Julianne leapt up from the table and put her arms first around Uncle Charlie, and then around Aunt Debbie. "He wants to see me, he wants to see me!" she cried into Aunt Debbie's neck.

"It is wonderful, dear," Aunt Debbie said, but Julianne thought she caught a hint of sadness in the woman's eyes. She brushed it off and ran out of the kitchen so she could go upstairs and pick out an outfit to wear for the following day.

* * *

The next day, Julianne was so excited she could barely concentrate on her studies. She was a little less than two weeks away from completing her senior year and obtaining her GED, and she couldn't wait to tell Stan all about it. Instead of working on her algebra, she planned out in her head what she was going to say to Stan.

First and foremost, she wanted to apologize. She would beg for his forgiveness and would cry until he gave it to her. Once she had that, she would tell him how miserable her life was since he had left her and that she wanted him back in her life. She would offer to be friends first, if that was what he wanted, especially since they were living several hours from each other, it may not be as easy to be together as it had been before. But if they could keep in touch by phone, then Julianne would apply to college in New Jersey the following year as she had always planned. Her life course was back in motion, and she trembled with excitement at the thought of Stan holding her in his big, strong arms once again. She longed to share the closeness that they had once had, and she knew that as long as she had him, she could finally fully accept the loss of her immediate family. Because to her, Stan was family.

Stan was the only family she would ever want for the rest of her life. Well, and Uncle Charlie and Aunt Debbie of course.

Blairstown, New Jersey

Julianne woke up on the morning of July 3, 1982, with a renewed sense of life. Although she now had brown hair she knew she looked just as beautiful as she had the day her and Stan first bumped into each other, and she put her outfit together painstakingly. Julianne carefully pulled out one of the new shirts that Aunt Debbie had purchased the other day. It was a red, short sleeved shirt with yellow piping around the sleeves, neck and waist. She matched it with her new ankle length peasant skirt with a red, blue and yellow pattern. Finally she put on the gold cross necklace that Stan had given her with the pearls throughout the chain. She applied her makeup carefully; not too much, she didn't want Stan to think she looked like the whore that he had broken up with. She wanted to make Stan's heart skip a beat; she wanted to make him miss her as much as she missed him.

After one last glance and smile in the mirror, she was ready. She blew her reflection a kiss and walked out of her bedroom into the kitchen, where Uncle Charlie and Aunt Debbie sat drinking coffee.

"Look at you, so pretty," Aunt Debbie smiled.

"I can't wait to see him," Julianne confessed. Aunt Debbie twisted her face into a weird contorted smile, scrunched up her eyes, and then looked away from Julianne and back at her husband.

"You all set?" Uncle Charlie asked. Julianne nodded excitedly. The first day of the rest of her life, she thought. Stan wouldn't have called and asked to see her if he didn't want to reconcile and get back together. At least that was what she was telling herself.

As she started to follow Uncle Charlie out of the kitchen, she noticed that Aunt Debbie hadn't moved from her seat. "Aunt Deb, aren't you coming?" Julianne asked. Aunt Debbie looked up at her, and Julianne noticed that her eyes looked slightly red-rimmed, like she had been crying.

"Can't, baby. Someone's dropping some stuff off here today, and I need to be here," Aunt Debbie said shakily.

"Is something wrong, Aunt Debbie?" Julianne asked, worriedly.

"No, sweetie, don't you worry. I'm fine. I'm just really happy that you and Stan are going to work things out and we're all going to be a family again," she said, her voice threatening to break with every word. Julianne was confused, but said thank you anyway.

Aunt Debbie finally got up out of her chair and came around the table to face Julianne. She pulled a wisp of Julianne's new shorter brown locks out of her mouth and smoothed her hair down, then she gave her a great big hug, squeezing her very tightly. Julianne hugged her back, still puzzled as to why Aunt Debbie was acting so strange. She figured she would ask Uncle Charlie in the car.

"Love you, Aunt Debbie," Julianne said, walking out the front door.

"Goodbye, my baby," Aunt Debbie said, shutting the door as they walked down the front steps toward the car. She could have sworn she heard Aunt Debbie completely break down once the door had been shut, but shook off the weird feeling, concentrated on winning Stan back, and got into the passenger seat of Uncle Charlie's blue Chevy. She put her seatbelt on and carefully smoothed out her skirt so it wouldn't have wrinkles when she got out.

"How long is it going to take us to get there?" Julianne asked Uncle Charlie as they pulled out of the driveway.

"Maybe two and a half hours, give or take," Uncle Charlie responded. "We're going to need to stop for gas before we get into the city."

They drove about forty minutes on the highway before Uncle Charlie pulled over into a gas station. As the attendant pumped their gas, Uncle Charlie got out of the car and went over to a pay phone to make a call. Julianne, figuring he was calling one of the girls for an appointment that night, giggled to herself and thanked God for getting her out of that life and into her new wonderful one.

Uncle Charlie seemed a bit nervous when he came back to the car, and Julianne asked him what was wrong.

"Oh, nothing," he waved her off. "One of the newer girls is giving me a little bit of trouble, that's all. Just had to call Dawn to have it straightened out."

"Did you tell Dawn where we were going?" Julianne asked him.

"Of course," Uncle Charlie said, smiling at her wryly out of the corner of his mouth. "She's very happy for you as well."

After a slight pause, Julianne asked, "Uncle Charlie, what was wrong with Aunt Debbie this morning?"

Uncle Charlie hesitated for a long moment, scrunched his brow, and then said, "Deb wants a baby. After all these years, we've never had any kids, and now that she's almost forty she finally wants a baby. I guess having you around the house made her realize that she wants kids after all."

"So, you guys are going to have a baby, then?" Julianne asked, concerned that a new baby in the house would affect her status as the beloved child of the Delgando household.

"I don't know," Charlie admitted gruffly. "Just something she's talking about. I'm near fifty, I don't know if I want a baby at all."

Julianne did not respond; she did not feel it was her business to pry any further.

After driving for another forty minutes or so, they were past Manhattan and into New Jersey. Julianne looked out the window and marveled at the sight of the factories and smokestacks; it was so different from her own local landscape. They drove for a while on the New Jersey Turnpike, and then Uncle Charlie got onto a smaller highway called Route 80.

"At the risk of sounding like an eight year old," Julianne joked, "Are we there yet?" She cast a sideways glance at Uncle Charlie only to see that he was sweating profusely. "What's wrong?" she asked, concerned.

"Hot in here," he said. Julianne had to admit, it was hot outside. And it seemed to be getting hotter the further away from the coast they drove. "We should be there in less than an hour," Uncle Charlie said.

Julianne continued to look out the windows, and before long the landscape changed again, back to the kind of scenery she was used to – trees and grass and flowers and suburban sights. At one point she saw a flash of silver in the side mirror and could have sworn it was

Dawn's car, but when she turned around the car was too far behind to see.

They passed signs that said Parsippany, and then Rockaway, and then Netcong. Finally, Julianne saw a sign that said "Hackettstown, 2 miles". Her heart leapt up in her throat and her hands immediately got clammy.

"There it is!" she sang.

"Yeah, there it is," Uncle Charlie said softly.

Julianne looked at the digital clock in the center dashboard. Only a little past one in the afternoon, she noted. She'd have plenty of time to spend the day with Stan before they would have to get going.

"What are you going to do while I'm with Stan?" Julianne asked Uncle Charlie.

His answer was short. "Don't know."

Just before they got to the exit, Uncle Charlie pulled off the highway into a scenic overlook. Julianne looked around and asked, "What are we doing here?"

"Need to breathe for a minute," Uncle Charlie said. He got out of the car and went around the back and opened the trunk. Julianne was baffled for what seemed like the millionth time that day. Why were they stopping so close to Hackettstown, when Stan was waiting for them? Why couldn't Uncle Charlie have just pulled over when they got there?

Julianne heard Uncle Charlie's footsteps in the gravel walking back around to the front of the car, and was startled when he suddenly showed up on her side of the car. Before she knew what was happening, Uncle Charlie opened the door and put a handkerchief over her nose and mouth. Julianne tried to struggle, but before she could even lift her arm to throw a punch, she slipped into unconsciousness and everything went black.

* * *

When Julianne awoke, she tried to open her mouth, but her facial functions had ceased to work. Her head felt like it weighed a thousand pounds, and when she tried to move it, she felt like it was going in slow motion. As she slowly regained consciousness, she realized she had a piece of fabric over her mouth, gagging her. She tried to move her hands but realized with horror that they had also been tied together with a soft fabric. Lastly, she tried to move her feet but finally grasped that they, too, had been bound. The smell of the chemical that Uncle Charlie had put over her face permeated her nostrils and she tried not to gag.

It took a few minutes for her to place where she was and remember what had happened, but it eventually came together. She knew that she was lying in the back seat of Uncle Charlie's Chevy and there was a flannel blanket over her. Though her face was covered, she could tell that it was dark outside. How long had she been out? She calculated at least seven or eight hours, seeing as it was just after one in the afternoon the last time she had looked at the clock. It suddenly came to her—she had been drugged.

Drugged.

Uncle Charlie had drugged her.

What was he doing? Where was he taking her? Where was Stan?

Several moments later, Julianne heard a voice speaking through the haze that surrounded her.

"I feel real bad about it, Dawn. It got too risky. She was a nice kid, but, I can't have her fucking up my life. I think she's real fucked up about what happened with Bob, and then her family, I think she's gonna tell someone."

Dawn?

"I know Charlie, I liked her too. I feel bad, she was a sweet girl."

Dawn was here? In the car? How did she get here?

"Debbie's all fucked up. Crying like crazy this morning when we left. Julianne asked me what was wrong, but I gave her some bullshit story."

He had lied about the baby story. So what was he doing with her?

"Charlie, I know this isn't something you usually do, but we just gotta do it and get rid of the body, and get the fuck out of here. We're far enough away from home. Her hair is a different color, nobody but us knows where she is, or even who she is. There isn't anyone left out there that will even know she's gone missing. By the time they find her, they won't even be able to ID her and we'll be home free."

Do it. Body. Find her. ID her.

Julianne nearly threw up all over the backseat as she finally realized what her "family" was up to. Uncle Charlie had taken her in as his own. Aunt Debbie had been crying this morning because she knew the misfortune that was about to befall her adopted daughter. Dawn had been her best friend and confidante.

They were all in it together.

They were going to kill her.

Once again she tried to move her hands, but to no avail. The combination of the drugs and the binding were no match for Julianne at the moment. She also didn't want them to hear her moving and figure out she was awake. She tried to think, but her brain was a black hole of fear, anger, and bewilderment as she tried to figure out exactly what she had done to warrant being killed.

"She totally bought the whole Stan story. It was kind of sad."

He had never even called, Julianne realized with a wave of sadness. *Stupid, stupid. He would have asked to talk to you if he had called, Julianne.*

She heard Dawn chuckle sarcastically. "She was a sad soul, that's for sure. Good thing there won't be a person in the country that will recognize her, or even miss her."

Tears stung Julianne's eyes as she heard her pseudo-sister talk so casually about her demise. For a moment, she accepted defeat, and thought that maybe it would just be better to join her mother and Sarah Jean in heaven.

But then with a renewed sense of anger she shifted, and the blanket fell off of her onto the floor. She slammed her eyes shut and hoped that they wouldn't notice. Her prayers were answered, Dawn and Uncle Charlie kept chattering away in the front seat. Julianne opened her eyes so she could barely see through the slits, and she saw Dawn sitting in the front seat, gesturing wildly with her hands, looking as perfect as ever.

"How fucking far are you going, Charlie? We're almost in Pennsylvania, you know."

"Shit, I don't want to go that far," Charlie said, putting on his right blinker. "You think there'll be a good enough spot here?" As they went underneath a road sign, Julianne saw that the sign read "Blairstown". Where the hell was Blairstown? Were they still in New Jersey?

She kept her eyes shut and slid around on the back seat, her mind whirling with possibilities. Maybe when they stopped the car she could just get up and run. But she couldn't open the door because her hands were bound, and she couldn't run because her feet were bound too. Julianne had not felt this helpless since that night with Bob...

She squeezed her eyes shut and tried to think. Maybe when they stopped the car she could cry out for help. Yes, that was it! There had to be people around, they were going to a town. To Blairstown. There had to be an abundance of people wherever they were going to stop, it wasn't like they were going to some remote place in the middle of nowhere. Julianne prayed that the ride would be over soon so she could get out and scream as loud as she could.

"How long do you think she'll stay out for?" Dawn asked.

"Not much longer," Charlie answered. "But hopefully long enough."

They were silent for the next few minutes, and then the car finally stopped. Neither Dawn nor Uncle Charlie moved for what felt like forever, and Dawn finally said, "Let's do this and get the hell out of here. I don't feel good."

Dawn's words slapped Julianne across the face like a cold wind. She still could not believe that this was her alleged best friend talking. Talking about killing her. When she got out of this alive, she was going to the police. She was going to rat out Uncle Charlie, and Dawn, and his whole operation. She hoped the police would protect her.

Dawn opened the passenger door and got out. As soon as she shut the door, she heard Uncle Charlie say something that sounded like, "I'm sorry, God", and then he also got out of the car.

She heard the trunk open and she heard objects being rustled around. She couldn't hear what Dawn and Uncle Charlie were saying but she could hear them talking in muffled tones. Julianne squeezed her eyes shut tightly as the trunk slammed shut and the side door opened. She lay absolutely still, and felt a warm breeze blow against the bottom of her bare feet. What had happened to her shoes? No time for that. Julianne breathed out of her mouth slowly and quietly and prepared herself for the massive scene that she was about to make.

Julianne felt a small hand grab her left ankle and heard a grunt as her body was pulled out the side door of the car. She knew it was Dawn because she could feel the girl's impeccably manicured fingernails digging into her skin. "Charlie, she's fucking heavy. Help me."

Julianne tried to stay as limp as she could. She felt another hand, with rougher skin, grab her wrists and pull her the rest of the way out of the car. Julianne collapsed in a heap outside the car. She could feel coarse grass underneath her, and before she opened her eyes she quickly counted to three in her head. The binding around her feet was not tight at all and had come somewhat loose, and Julianne felt certain that not only would she be able to yell, but she would also probably be able to run.

There was silence all around her, except for crickets chirping. *Where were the people?* Julianne wondered. *Why didn't she hear anyone?*

She knew it was now or never. Adrenaline pumping, just as she thought she was about to lose her nerve, she thrust her eyes open and clumsily stood up. The rag fell off her feet with ease, and she shook her head violently from side to side, shaking the gag off her face. She started shrieking and screaming for help.

"Holy fucking shit, she's awake!" Dawn exclaimed. "Charlie!"

Julianne's eyes bulged as she looked into Dawn's frightened face, and she attempted to will her feet to start running. She looked around wildly, trying to determine which way showed signs of safety. She felt a sickening feeling in the pit of her stomach as she realized they were in the middle of a field. There were no people. There were no cars. There was no road. There weren't even any lights, aside from the interior light of Uncle Charlie's car. She heard rustling in the grass from behind the car, and suddenly saw Uncle Charlie lumbering toward her with a baseball bat.

Julianne heard Dawn start sobbing softly as she watched Uncle Charlie quickly wind up and bring the bat behind his head.

RUN!

She lifted up a foot, but the drugs were still emanating throughout her system, and her legs felt like lead.

RUN!

She put her foot down on the jagged, dead grass and attempted to pick up the other one. At the same time she watched in horror as Uncle Charlie began to swing the bat directly at her face.

Julianne felt and heard the sickening crack at the same time. It hurt worse than Stan dumping her, worse than the heartwrenching loss of her beloved sister, and way worse than the night she had been anally raped by Bob. For the second time in less than six months, Julianne felt blood gush from her nose. Her eyes rolled back in her head and she started choking on the warm liquid that was slowly filling the back of her throat. She fell against the Chevy and slid down on the grass.

"Is she dead?" Dawn shrieked, horrified, staring at Julianne's lifeless body.

Julianne started to make a gurgling noise and her eyes fluttered uncontrollably.

"Mother fucker," Uncle Charlie cursed under his breath.

As Julianne writhed on the grass, she opened her eyes wide just in time to see Uncle Charlie wind up with the bat once again.

She tried to call out, but her throat and mouth were full of blood. Just as she let out another bloody gurgle, Uncle Charlie brought the bat down again.

The next thing Julianne saw was Sarah Jean's smiling face.

Princess Doe

J ames Harter was in the middle of a dream when he heard the phone ring. He stirred slowly, hoping it was part of his delusion, when he heard it again, shrill and demanding.

He opened his eyes and looked at the clock. Seven twenty in the morning. Who was calling him at this ungodly hour on his day off? His young wife Charlotte stirred next to him.

The phone rang again, demanding to be answered. James flung his arm out, yanked the phone off the receiver, and mumbled, "'Lo?"

"Harter." James heard his boss's gruff voice on the other end of the line. "McCallahan here. We found a body. Cemetery on Route 94. Get here now." There was a click as the line went dead.

It took a minute for James' brain to register what his boss, Sergeant Patrick McCallahan, had just said. When it sank in, he sat up sharply in bed, rubbing the sleep out of his eyes.

"What happened, baby?" Charlotte murmured next to him.

James shook his head. A body? In Blairstown? How could that be? Nothing happened in Blairstown. Besides the fact that it had a small population of 3,900, most of whom had been family friends for decades, it was one of the safest places in New Jersey.

James Harter got dressed with a sick feeling in his stomach, almost certain that he would know the person whose body he was about to go investigate. He had grown up in Blairstown and he and Charlotte knew pretty much every young woman in the area.

"They found a body," James said softly as he pulled on his cotton blue police slacks.

Charlotte sat up in bed, startled. "A body?" she queried. "Whose?"

"I don't know, Charlotte," James answered. He hated when his wife asked questions. He was twenty-six and had only been on the police force for a year, and still had a hard time drawing the line between confidentiality and family.

"Well what did they say?" she prodded.

"They didn't. I'll call you as soon as I know more." With a kiss on the forehead, James left his disoriented wife in bed and walked out of the house, grabbing his police cruiser keys off the key hanger as he exited.

James pulled into the iron gates of the Cedar Ridge Cemetery, waving at the officer who was stationed by the street. He followed the gravel road until he saw two other police cruisers, and then parked his car and got out.

He saw McCallahan about ten yards away, farther into the field, talking to another officer and shaking his head. Striding toward his boss, he prayed again that he would not know the victim.

"Who is it?" he asked McCallahan as soon as his boss looked him in the eye.

"We have no idea," McCallahan said somberly. "It's a young girl. Brown hair, teenager, face bludgeoned and badly decomposed."

"Who found her?" James asked.

"Caretaker," Mc Callahan answered. "He's over there. Go talk to him, he's a bit shaken up."

James looked in the direction of the elderly caretaker, who was sitting on a bench, shaking his head. He walked over to him and introduced himself.

"I was just....mowing," the old man said. "And then, by the stones over there, I found her. I thought maybe she was just passed out drunk, so I called out to her, but she didn't move. Then when I got closer I saw that she was...bloody...and...blue."

James instantly felt sorry for the old man. He was just doing his job, on a calm summer morning, and had come across a gruesome discovery that he didn't ask to be a part of.

"Did you touch the body?" he asked the caretaker.

"No," the man replied, "As soon as I saw that she wasn't breathing, I went back to the office and called the cops."

"How long ago was that?"

"Half hour ago or so."

James followed the caretaker's gaze to the scene of the crime, and saw that someone had already covered the girl's body with a piece of tarp.

"Thank you, sir," he said.

The old man shook his head. "She can't be more than seventeen," he said sadly. "Can't even tell what she looks like, poor girl."

James left the caretaker and went over to investigate the body for himself. The crime photographer was already there, snapping pictures of the surrounding area. Harter went up to Officer Markman, who was writing in a pad, and asked him, "Can I see it?"

Markman looked at the young officer standing before him. Harter didn't have to say that he had never seen a dead body before; being on the police force in Blairstown for only a year, everyone knew. Police officers that had been on the force for ten years hadn't ever seen a body. Things like this just didn't happen in Blairstown.

"Wear these gloves," Markman said, shoving a pair of latex gloves into James' arms. James put on the gloves and cautiously walked over to the black tarp. He saw a stiff, pallid foot sticking out of the plastic, and swallowed the urge to retch. Markman watched as Harter slowly picked up the tarp and surveyed the body.

James' eyes instantly filled with tears as he inspected the loss of life in front of him. Her torso was twisted, her knees were slightly bent, and her arms were on either side of her, palms up. The clothes that she was wearing were dirty and covered in blood, mostly her shirt. The bottoms of her feet were dirty, and James noticed she was not wearing shoes and there were none anywhere in sight. A gold cross necklace fell just above her hardened breastbone. James noticed the pearls that were inlaid in the chain. As his eyes made their way up to her face, he once again nearly gagged. The poor girl had barely anything left above her neck, save for her brown hair. He vaguely made out the crushed outline of a nose, and her lips seemed to be pushed more to the left side of her head. The girl's right eye was open, revealing a socket that had been eaten by maggots, but her left eye had been completely mangled and bashed in. There was a massive dent in her forehead, and James could see pieces of her skull poking out.

Whoever killed this girl had blatantly slammed her face multiple times; an obvious attempt for the police not to be able to identify her. The killer's attempt had worked. James figured between the damage and the decomposition, it would be very difficult to piece together what this girl's face had looked like before she met her untimely death.

He turned around and called to Markman, "How long you think she's been here?"

"Two weeks, maybe slightly less," Markman called back, still scribbling in his notebook.

"Who is she?" James asked the question that was on everyone's mind.

No one answered.

James closed his eyes and tried to picture the girl before she had died. He saw a vibrant beauty with flawless skin and sky blue eyes, full of life and smiling brightly.

"It won't take long to solve this," James heard Mc Callahan say. "Young girl like this, she's got to have a family, and in such a small area….there aren't many possibilities. We've already got headquarters running data on all the missing girls in the tri-state area."

James opened his eyes and saw a news van pull up in the distance and park on the side of Route 94. He saw the news crew get out and run toward the gates of the cemetery like sharks at a feeding.

"For now we'll call her Jane Doe," Markman said, still scrawling away in his notepad.

"Jane Doe," said Mc Callahan. "Sounds good. We'll find out her name before long, I'm sure."

James heard himself speaking up, frightened because of his rookie status. But he felt compelled to speak on behalf of this nameless being, with whom he had made an unexplained connection in the five minutes that he had knelt by her side. "No," he said.

"What was that, Harter?" Mc Callahan barked.

"She's more than that," James said, brushing the matted hair off her mangled face with his gloved hand. "She's more than a Jane. She's a princess."

"Harter, what the hell are you talking about?" Mc Callahan snarled again.

James was vaguely aware that the news crew was less than twenty-five feet away. He looked at them half-heartedly as he slowly rotated his head to his boss.

"She deserves more than Jane. Let's call her Princess Doe," James heard himself saying.

"Fine," Mc Callahan said. "Princess Doe. It'll probably sound better in the news anyway."

James looked at the stiffened Princess Doe lying motionless on the dead grass in front of him. Using one of his latex-covered hands, he carefully closed her one open eye with all the respect he could muster.

"Don't worry, Princess Doe," he whispered to the corpse that was sprawled out before his very eyes, "I promise, with every breath in my body, we will find your killer. And of course, without question, your identity will be revealed as soon as possible."

Harter heard a raucous noise behind him, and gently replaced the tarp over Princess Doe, being sure to cover the errant foot that had been sticking out earlier.

Taking a deep breath, he stood up and turned around to the sound of reporters shouting out questions and cameras clicking away.